Sally's first instinct was to drive away.

But Colin was already walking towards her car. He had on jeans and an old—a very old—University of Alberta sweatshirt. She'd probably seen him in that sweatshirt a hundred times.

Including, if memory served her correctly, that one fateful night over sixteen years ago...

When Colin was close enough to touch her car, she lowered the passenger-side window.

For a moment they just looked at each other, and in his eyes she recognised the sorrow that she'd been feeling.

She also saw that he was concerned about her. But there was something else she couldn't name. It was like a spark, alive and glowing. And it reminded her that despite how she felt at times, she was a woman with half her life still in front of her.

Available in August 2006
from Silhouette Superromance

A Little Secret
Between Friends

CJ CARMICHAEL

SILHOUETTE®
*Super*ROMANCE™

*First published in Great Britain 2006
Silhouette Books, Eton House, 18-24 Paradise Road,
Richmond, Surrey TW9 1SR*

© Carla Daum 2005

Standard ISBN 0 373 71277 4
Promotional ISBN 0 373 60491 2

38-0806

*Printed and bound in Spain
by Litografia Rosés S.A., Barcelona*

Dear Reader,

A difficult moral dilemma is at the heart of many stories I write. This story is no different.

Imagine you are a student in your last year of university. There's this guy who has been in many of your classes…and something about him really gets to you. He's good-looking, charming and way too smart for his own good. You keep wanting to show him up. Then one night you're at the library late at night together and he offers you a ride home. Sparks fly, and before you know it, this guy you thought you couldn't stand is someone you just can't resist.

The next morning you check in with your roommate and best friend. Before you can tell her what happened last night, she tells you about this guy she really likes—and it's your guy!

Do you tell her to back off? Or do you leave the field clear for your friend?

In the story you're about to read, Sally Stowe faced just this situation. Sally decided to date someone else and leave the guy for her friend… and the repercussions of that decision still live with her—and her daughter—sixteen years later.

I hope you enjoy this story. If you would like to write or send e-mail, I would be delighted to hear from you through my website at www.cjcarmichael. com. Or send mail to the following Canadian address: #1754-246 Stewart Green SW, Calgary, Alberta, T3H 3C8, Canada.

Sincerely,

CJ Carmichael

For sharing her knowledge of family law and the challenges of juggling a career with motherhood, I thank Sandra J Hildebrand, barrister and solicitor.

Thanks also to Joe Nolan, retired RCMP officer, and Terry Evenson, Executive Director of the Canadian Bar Association of Alberta (and also a lovely aunt!).

CHAPTER ONE

"BE CAREFUL with that knife, Sal. You wouldn't want to hurt yourself."

Sally Stowe froze. The unexpected sound of her ex-husband's voice had a similar effect to a steel blade running lightly down her spine.

Keeping her back to him, she resumed chopping the red pepper with precise, measured slices. She took a beat to catch her breath, then said coolly, "We have this custom in North America, Neil. It's called knocking before you enter a home that isn't your own."

Though her exterior was unruffled—she hoped!—her mind raced. Why was Neil here? He knew Lara was on a birthday sleepover party tonight. Sally had learned long ago to get his permission for every single thing Lara did. If she so much as booked a dentist appointment without his approval, Neil would turn ballistic.

"The door was unlocked."

As if that were an excuse. Still, it was a good reminder to be more careful. Sally crouched to reassure the six-month-old puppy whining anxiously at her feet—the cause of the unlocked door. He needed to go out so often she'd become lazy with the dead bolt, which would only engage if you aligned the door just shy of fully closed.

"It's okay, Armani." She gave the mutt a scratch behind his ears, then patted him on the side gently.

Strangers—and Neil—made the poor thing nervous.

In his most scornful voice, Neil said, "Armani? Who calls a dog after a fashion designer, for God's sake?"

Still avoiding eye contact with him, Sally did her best to answer calmly. "Your daughter." And he, of all people, ought to know why. He was the one who had fostered Lara's taste for expensive, designer clothing—although even Neil drew the line at Armani, fortunately.

"Well, the dog's black, at least."

Yes. And with the patch of white on his chest, he looked a little like he was wearing a tux. But Sally didn't share that piece of trivia with Neil. She shared nothing with her ex-husband that wasn't required in their joint-custody agreement.

An agreement that she, as a lawyer, understood inside and out. Neil, also a lawyer, knew the agreement equally well, since he had drafted it.

As Sally went to the sink to rinse her hands, she glanced out the window at the thawing April landscape. The grass was still brown, but there would be pussy willows soon. Chunks of ice were breaking up in the river that bordered the western edge of her property.

She'd moved here, to the Elbow Valley community on the outskirts of Calgary, two years ago when Lara had turned fourteen. Sally was determined to keep her young teenager away from the influences of shopping malls, corner stores and video arcades, where Sally knew trouble could be found as easily as a super-size Slurpee.

Their stone-faced bungalow was one of the smaller homes in the estate neighborhood, but it sat on a full acre of land, backing onto the Elbow River. Sally reveled in the fact that they weren't even considered part of the city of Calgary, though she was only a twenty-five minute commute from the office.

The country setting was perfect, but the isolation did make her nervous at times, which was why she'd finally given in to Lara's desire for a dog. Hopefully one day Armani would develop some guarding instincts. The woman at the animal shelter had been sure he was mostly border collie, a breed known to be both protective and gentle with children.

Sally turned off the water and moved to the stove, situated on the island at the center of the kitchen. She unhooked the wok from the overhead rack and settled it on the front burner. After twisting the knob to high heat, she finally lifted her head to acknowledge Neil's presence.

Her ex-husband still stood near the door. The family room lay to his left, the kitchen to the right. "Are you going to invite me in, Sal? Looks like you have enough food for two."

He was right about the food. Out of habit she'd prepared enough for Lara, as well, even though her daughter was out. But if she had food for twenty, she'd never invite Neil to her table.

"What do you want? Did you forget Lara is sleeping over at Jessica's tonight?"

"Can't a man stop by for a friendly visit with his ex-wife?" Neil smiled, managing to look boyishly attractive, even though, like her, he'd passed forty.

He was a debonair man, her ex-husband. Medium height, slender, he wore a suit really well. His hair was dark and thick, and the lingering trace of his English accent added to his misleading appeal.

"But actually, I've brought over Lara's passport application papers for you to sign." He placed them, plus his silver pen, the one she'd given him for Christmas on Lara's behalf, on the island.

Sally leaned over and pulled the documents closer. Neil's father, who had worked in investment banking, had brought his family to Canada for the two years he'd been stationed to work in Calgary. When the upper executive had had a massive heart attack and died, Neil's mother had returned to Kent. Neil, who'd been accepted to law school at the University of Alberta, had remained.

This summer Neil planned to take Lara to visit his mother. Sally hated the idea of their daughter making an overseas trip without her, but she couldn't deny Lara the chance to get to know her one surviving grandparent.

She executed the distinctive loop at the end of Stowe, then dropped the pen. "There."

Neil folded the pages and stuffed them into the breast pocket of his jacket. "I see you've poured yourself a glass of wine. Drinking alone, Sal?"

The open bottle sat on the counter behind her, next to the cutting board with the diced chicken, peppers and onions. But Sally ignored both it and Neil's question. She'd given him what he wanted. It was time for him to leave. To her dismay, though, he sidled along the island. Moving closer.

"Come on, Sal. Let's drink a toast to your good news. What?" One eyebrow arched in casual question. "You didn't think I knew that my ex-wife is the front-runner to replace Judge Kendal on the bench?"

Oh, no, he'd heard the rumors. She should have guessed he would have. And that he'd be quick to react. Her professional accomplishments always triggered Neil's worst displays of temper. Too late she wished she'd lied about dinner and said she was expecting company. Neil would never buy the story now. Especially since she'd set only one plate at the counter. Taken down just the single wineglass.

Maybe she could improvise…

"Neil, you really need to be going. I have to eat quickly. My book club is meeting here at seven." That was only half an hour from now. And a smart man like Neil would factor in the possibility that someone might arrive early…

"Sal." He gave her a disappointed smile. "Don't you think I know you meet with your book club on the *second* Friday of every month? Not the third."

"We had to change for April," she said, doing her best to speak slowly. "Because of spring break."

"I don't think so. You always were a lousy liar. But that's probably a good thing. Judges shouldn't lie, should they, Sal?"

"You're getting ahead of yourself, Neil. Willa isn't retiring for another two months. And I'm sure there are other worthy candidates for the position." Sally couldn't be sure she would get the appointment until she had the official call from the federal justice minister.

"Who do you think you're fooling with that bogus humility? Not me, I assure you."

He had that smile on his face now. Beth had called

it the ice-man smile. He used it in court occasionally when he was moving in for the kill on a vulnerable witness. But to Sally the ice-man smile never
seemed as cruel, as ruthless, as when she felt it di-
rected at herself.

"Whatever, Neil."

"Justice Stowe. Sounds very distinguished,
doesn't it?"

"Neil—"

"Long-term board member of that stupid battered
women's shelter. Past president of the law society.
The volunteer hours in dispute resolutions. Looks
like all your goody-goody work is actually paying
off."

With each word, Sally could sense his anger
building. There was no avoiding a full-scale argument now, she knew from experience. Any word, any
movement, even a facial twitch on her part could set
him off. Might as well get it over with, she decided.

"That's right. It's all paying off. With any luck,
in two months I'm going to be appointed to the
bench. Is that why you dropped by tonight—to offer
your congratulations?"

The changes that fell over his face were utterly
predictable. First his eyebrows lowered into a frown.
His smile tightened. His eyes narrowed.

He moved again, rounding the island and then
cornering her against the counter.

"Congratulations?" He spit out the word. "You think you deserve a pat on the back for reneging on your real job—raising our child and being a good wife?"

"I'm not your wife anymore."

"To me you are. I may have signed those papers…."

He'd had to sign them. She'd known him well enough to serve them when he was at work, in a meeting. He couldn't pretend to his colleagues that nothing was amiss. So he'd pretended, instead, that the divorce was his idea. She didn't care about that. All she'd wanted was to finally be legally free of the man.

Except she wasn't free. Would never be free. Not as long as they shared custody of Lara. Neil had their daughter alternate weekends and every Wednesday evening. He'd pick her up from dry-land training at Canada Olympic Park, take her out for dinner, then bring her home around nine.

"To me, you'll always be mine. You're still sexy, Sal. In some ways even more than when you were in your twenties. What do you say, babe? Maybe we should celebrate your good news in bed."

She couldn't stop herself from cringing. The memories of times in their marriage when she'd made love with him in order to avoid a fight came back in a rush of shame. Why had she married so quickly? So thoughtlessly?

With hindsight, none of her reasons seemed compelling enough to warrant landing herself with Neil Anderson for the rest of her life.

"Don't look at me that way. I remember when you couldn't get enough in the sack. But now that you're about to become a judge, you're too good for me. Is that it, Sal?"

He'd moved to within touching distance. Armani started whining again.

"Get out of my face, Neil. You may be scaring the dog, but you're not scaring me. Those days are long over."

He could scream and yell and rant at her as long as he liked. She didn't care. As long as he was mad about something that didn't affect Lara, it simply didn't matter.

That's what Sally told herself, but her body refused to take the presence of an angry, hulking man in her kitchen quite so lightly. She could feel all the old warning signs. Racing heart, damp palms, shallow breathing. She forced herself to fill her lungs with air and release it slowly.

Neil watched her face with the fascination of a scientist observing slides under a microscope. "You're a coldhearted bitch. You've been judging men for years. Now you'll get to do it in court. Break their balls and send them to jail for as long as the law allows. God help the slobs who look for mercy from you."

Sally didn't listen to the words. She was used to Neil's diatribes. He had several favorite themes, from her dearth of maternal instincts for their daughter, to her hatred of men in general, and him in particular. She was frigid, a bitch, and worse...

At some point he'd start swearing and then he'd throw something, maybe punch a wall, and leave.

But tonight he was frighteningly calm and still.

And close.

He was a fanatically clean man, but he could not hide his own essence beneath the scent of his soap, his aftershave, his mouthwash. That essence, as familiar to her as his every expression, made her ill.

Yet, she refused to back away. She lifted her gaze and stared him straight in the eyes, not caring if he saw the contempt she felt in her heart.

"You always thought you were too good for me, Sal, didn't you? Right from the beginning."

Though his words were uttered quietly, his jaw was tight. She saw a sheen of moisture on his brow, noticed his fist clench at his side.

"Get out of my house, Neil."

"*Your* house? *YOUR* house?"

His eyes glazed over and Sally knew this was it. He was gone. If any sliver of logic could have reached him before, now it was no longer possible. She watched him lift his hand. The wine bottle was nearby. She knew the way he thought, the way he operated. He was going to break the bottle, hurl it onto the tile flooring, or worse, throw it across the room.

Red wine was going to be spilled all over her beautiful, spanking-new kitchen…

But Neil's hand didn't stop at the bottle. It kept moving and just a split second before she went flying, she realized the hand was headed for her.

He pushed her violently, letting loose a barrage of cursing at the same time.

"No!" Feeling herself lose her balance, Sally threw out her arms. One hand glanced off the wok, the smoking, hot wok.

She hollered in pain, and then he shoved her again, harder this time. She felt her legs fly out from under her. On the way down her head glanced off the edge of the granite counter with a thud.

For a second all was numb. Then sensation returned in an explosion of pain.

Oh, God!

She landed on the floor, on the cold, hard tile and couldn't stop herself from moaning. Her head vibrated with waves of pain. She couldn't believe she was still conscious. She put a hand to the spot and felt the warm stickiness of blood.

"Neil…" she moaned. *Phone the ambulance,* she wanted to say, but she couldn't get out the words. *Oh, my head, my head. Help me, Neil. Surely you didn't mean to do this.*

"You always were clumsy in the kitchen, Sal."

She couldn't see him, but she felt his breath in her ear as he spoke the words. He must be crouching on the floor beside her. Sally tried to open her eyes, but all she saw was darkness. White dots of light.

"You're never going to be a judge, you bitch. When I'm finished with you, you'll be lucky if you aren't disbarred."

She heard his pants rustle as he stood and she had a sudden fear of being kicked. She was so vulnerable here on the floor, writhing at his feet. She forced herself to be still, to stop the moaning. No matter that she could hardly breathe for the throbbing in her head. She couldn't let him see her broken.

Seconds ticked by. She waited for his next move. A kick? A punch? Would he throw something at her?

And then she heard his hard-soled shoes clapping on the Mediterranean tile floor. The sound receded, then stopped. The back door opened, slammed shut.

He was gone. Thank goodness he was gone.

She curled her legs up toward her chest and tried to lift her head. No. Impossible.

Armani's paws clacked against the tile as he came to check her out. She felt his soft, warm tongue on her hand.

"Good boy," she tried to whisper.

Blackness. Pain. The smell of blood.

Have to get up. But she couldn't. Armani continued to whine, to nudge her hand with his nose.

Ow. Her burned hand hurt. Everything hurt. *Need help.*

Beth.

With her uninjured hand, she pulled out the cell phone clipped to her waist. Her thumb passed over the buttons, pressing a familiar speed-dial number by rote.

Her fingers were slick with blood, her movements uncoordinated. The phone slipped to the floor near her head. The house was so quiet, she could hear the rings. One. Two. Three.

Someone answered. It was a man's voice. That was wrong. She didn't want a man.

Beth. She tried to speak, but didn't know if any sound came out. *Help me, Beth.*

Then all went dark.

CHAPTER TWO

CROWN PROSECUTOR Colin Foster was home watching the hockey game when the phone rang. He'd boiled himself some bacon-and-onion perogies for dinner, and a plate smeared with sour cream sat on his footstool next to a half-empty beer.

The Flames had made the playoffs and were into overtime with the Canucks to tie the series. He didn't want to answer the damn call, but when he leaned over and saw the name on display, his priorities took a sudden shift.

Sally Stowe. Why was she phoning? He couldn't think of a single reason. But there were plenty why she wouldn't.

He hit mute on the remote control. His study went bizarrely silent as the action continued on the big-screen TV. Leaning forward in his leather chair, he pressed the talk button.

"Hello?"

Nothing. Then some muffled, indistinguishable noises.

"Sally, is that you?" Was that a sob? "Are you all right?"

More muffled noises, barely discernible as words. And then one word, very faintly. "Beth."

"Sally?" Why was she asking for his wife? What was going on?

But there was only silence from the line.

Colin waited for several seconds, maybe even a whole minute. When nothing else happened, he finally hung up and tried to think of explanations. Sally had been his wife's best friend. In the past she would phone here all the time.

But not at all for the past six months.

Had she dialed the number by mistake? He could see that happening, easily enough. But Sally would have apologized as soon as she'd realized her error.

And what about those background noises? And that soft cry of *"Beth…"*

Something must be wrong. Sally's place wasn't far. He'd better drive over and make sure she and Lara were all right.

Colin turned off the TV, then grabbed Beth's key chain from the hall. He was pretty sure his wife had kept a spare for Sally's house. They used to water plants and bring in mail when either one went on a trip without the other.

Best friends. Yes, they'd been best friends all right. For as long as he'd known them, they'd been closer than sisters. They celebrated birthdays together, went on annual girl-holidays and dyed each other's hair. They'd even decided to move into the same neighborhood so they would be close to each other.

Colin hadn't minded. He was happy with the Elbow Valley home he and Beth had selected. And the community, with its network of biking trails, connected green spaces, and a frozen pond for skating in the winter, would have been a perfect place to raise kids.

If he and Beth had only managed to have them.

Colin went through the laundry room to the three-car garage, hitting the power button for the door opener on his way to the SUV.

As he passed the Miata convertible Beth had loved so much, he felt a twinge of guilt. There was so much he'd let slide this last while. He knew the registration on the Miata was expired, and so was the insurance, probably. Beth's clothes were still in her closet, her mail unopened. Hell, he was pretty sure there was a container of her yogurt in the back of the fridge. Probably more mold than yogurt by now.

He had to start dealing with all this. Pull together the pieces that were left of his life. As he backed his vehicle out of the garage, Colin made a promise to himself. He was going to make a list and get busy.

Soon. Very soon.

Not tonight, but tomorrow for sure. First he had to find out why Sally Stowe was calling a woman who had been dead for six months.

SALLY WASN'T SURE how long she'd lain on the floor—fifteen minutes? Maybe twenty?—when she heard knocking at the front door.

Not Neil, was her first coherent thought. He would have just barged in.

So then, who? She wasn't expecting anyone. Maybe a canvasser or something.

She tried to sit up, then moaned. Her head hurt so much, she must have a concussion. But her injuries couldn't be too serious. She was conscious and her mind was working all right. Wasn't it? Let's see, she was Sally Stowe and today was April the twenty-third and the capital of Alberta was... Edmonton.

Yes, she was fine, she was absolutely fine. If only she could pick herself up from the floor.

There was another knock, this one at the kitchen door. For a second she panicked. Maybe it *was* Neil, checking if she was alive.

Or making sure she wasn't...

Armani whined, and she put a reassuring hand on his back. She wished someone could do the same for her. Neil had never been physically violent before. She didn't know what to make of it.

The door opened. A voice called out, "Sally? Are you home?"

Not Neil. Relief was quickly replaced by a different kind of alarm. What was Colin Foster doing here? The island blocked him from her view and it worked vice versa, as well. If she kept quiet, maybe he would leave. She certainly didn't want him to see her this way.

On the hand, she could use some help.

In the end, the decision wasn't Sally's to make. Colin entered the kitchen. He must have seen the blue flame on the stove, because he came rushing around the island and almost tripped over her.

"Oh my God, Sally! What happened to you?"

He crouched beside her, as Neil had done, only this time she felt no fear. Armani seemed to sense his presence was benign, as well. He stopped whining and lay down at Sally's side.

"My head," she said, barely finding the strength to speak. "My hand." She lifted it slightly.

"You burned yourself." Colin reached to the stove and switched off the burner. "Badly. And you've hit your head. It's still bleeding."

He opened drawers until he found the clean tea towels. Taking several, he made a compress and applied it to her wound. He tied one of the towels completely around her head to hold the others in place.

Then he found a bowl, filled it with cold water

and immersed her burned hand. The relief from pain was instantaneous.

"Talk to me, Sally. Are you okay?"

"I'm fine. My name is Sally Elizabeth Stowe and it's Friday the twenty-third."

He looked taken aback at first, and then he smiled. "Well, your mind is working all right. But then it always has."

This, coming from a man who had spent the past decade and a half debating almost everything she said, was a compliment, Sally knew.

"What a lot of blood."

His face was awfully white, Sally noticed. He'd aged since Beth's death, but not unattractively. A little gray sprinkled in with the chestnut-brown. A few more lines spreading out from the corners of his alert, probing eyes.

"Head injuries always bleed profusely, Colin." She remembered Lara, when she was two, splitting her head open on the stone hearth of their first rental home, and the amazing amount of blood she'd lost in a relatively short time. Sally had hit the panic button then, but at Emergency Lara had received three stitches and been pronounced fine.

On the drive home, Neil had bitterly castigated Sally for her carelessness, conveniently forgetting that she had asked him to keep an eye on Lara while she folded the laundry.

That had been the last in a series of arguments that had convinced her she could not spend a lifetime with the man she'd married so rashly. She'd moved out the next week. Drawn up a separation agreement that Neil had never signed...

"Must have been a hell of a fall, Sally. Did you burn your hand, then lose your balance?"

She closed her eyes, remembering the vile sneer on Neil's face just before he'd given her that second shove. The ice-man smile.

She doubted if any of Neil's colleagues would believe that the polished, urbane man who was one of the city's most accomplished criminal lawyers had this darker side.

Besides, even if Colin did believe her, she wasn't sure she wanted him to know.

"That must be what happened. It's all kind of blurry right now."

Blurry was the right word. Her vision still wasn't quite right. And her understanding of the situation was equally out of focus. Neil had lost his temper hundreds of times before, but he'd never laid a hand on her before. What was so different this time? Did he resent her possible judicial appointment that much?

"You look like you're in a lot of pain."

"I'm actually starting to feel a little better."

"You'll need stitches for that cut, I'm guessing."

He was probably right.

"Should I call an ambulance?"

"I'm not that badly off. But maybe you could drop me at the Rockyview Emergency? Unless you have plans?"

Colin's laugh was bitter. "I never have plans these days. Not that it would matter if I did. Come on, sweetheart, we've got to get you up off that floor."

He started to put his arms under her then paused.

"You smell good," she murmured.

"What?"

She couldn't believe she'd said that. It was just the contrast from Neil, she supposed. "Don't mind me. I'm delirious."

"Before I move you I'd better make sure you don't have any other injuries. Back? Neck?"

"Fine. Nothing hurts but my head and my hand." And those were enough. "You know, a few painkillers would go down real nice about now."

"Let's get you up, first. Here goes." Colin put his arms under her back, helping her to a sitting position. "Okay?"

"A little dizzy," she admitted.

"Think you can make it to the car?"

"But all this blood will stain your seats." There was a pool of the stuff in the kitchen. It was on her shirt and Colin's socks. He must have removed his shoes at the door.

"I'll take care of it," Colin promised. "What about the dog?"

"Could you put him in the laundry room, please?"

Colin pulled off his socks so he wouldn't track blood all over her house, then settled the dog. Next he grabbed a throw blanket from the family room and wrapped it around her shoulders. As gently as possible, he helped her up. Slowly they crossed to the back door where he slipped his shoes back onto his feet, then swung her up into his arms and carried her out to his car.

The round trip to the emergency room took under four hours, which wasn't as bad as it could have been. Colin stuck with her the whole time, except when she was in the examining room.

"How many stitches?" he asked on the drive home.

She fingered the raw spot on the side of her head. "Four. You know, I've never had stitches before. If you don't count childbirth."

"Why would you…?" Colin began to ask. Then, "Oh…" as he figured the answer out on his own. "That must really hurt."

"It's not the worst part," she assured him, then smiled at his grimace.

It was peaceful riding in the car with Colin, which was strange. She wasn't used to being in his vicinity without a good argument brewing between them.

Usually legal in nature, but sometimes political or economic. In truth, their world views weren't that different, but from the first time they'd butted heads in law school, they'd seemed to take pleasure in picking fights with each other.

Back at her house, Colin surprised her by producing a key to her front door, then helping her inside. When she looked at him questioningly, he said, "It's Beth's." He started to work it off the chain, but she stopped him.

"Keep it. If I ever lock myself out, I'll be glad you have the spare."

Trailing her hand along the hallway wall, to keep herself steady, Sally headed for the laundry room. As soon as she opened the door, Armani tumbled out, barking excitedly.

"I'll take care of him. You should get some rest." Colin crouched beside the puppy. "I'll bet you need to go outside, don't you, fella?"

"Thank you, Colin." Sally couldn't wait to get off her feet. It was almost midnight now and all she wanted was sleep. In the hospital Colin had told her he would stay the night to keep an eye on her. Otherwise, the doctor would have insisted on admitting her.

Sally tossed her bloodied clothing into the hamper and put on flannel pajamas. She managed to brush her teeth then, with relief, crawled under the covers.

Within a minute, she heard Armani and Colin return to the house. There were some noises in the laundry room. She presumed Colin was making sure the puppy had food and water for the night.

Then Colin came to her room. She'd left the door open, but he stood out in the hall.

"Are you okay?"

"Fine." The painkillers were blessedly effective.

"How long were you there? Lying on the floor before I got here."

"I'm not sure. Lucky for me you showed up when you did." Then she realized how strange that was. Colin *never* dropped by, and certainly wouldn't do so without phoning first. "How was it you came for a visit tonight, anyway?"

Colin looked surprised. "Don't you remember phoning?" He disappeared down the hall, returning a few minutes later with her cell phone. He'd wiped off the blood and now he pressed a button to show her the last number dialed.

She vaguely recalled fumbling with her cell phone, then dropping it. "I must have hit one of the speed-dial buttons."

"When I answered you asked for Beth."

"Oh." Now that he said that, she recalled thinking of her friend in those first painful and confusing moments. Beth had always been the person she turned to during an emergency.

But how awful for him, to get a call like that. "I'm sorry, Colin. I guess it must have been instinct or something. I wasn't thinking straight."

"That's okay." He disappeared down the hall, then came back with painkillers and a glass of water.

"You make a good nurse," she told him, and immediately regretted the words. Beth had died at home and that last month had been hard. There'd been professional home care, but both Colin and Sally had helped. Then, the last two weeks they'd taken turns so Beth would never be alone.

He'd made a good nurse then, too.

"I keep saying the wrong thing." Was it her injury? Or just being around Colin? He'd always brought out the worst in her. In law school she'd been compelled to prove him wrong at every opportunity. And when they occasionally found themselves on opposite sides of the same courtroom, sparks were sure to fly. They were so combustible they'd earned a reputation with their colleagues.

But there'd been no hint of an argument between them tonight.

"That's okay, Sally. But it was hell seeing her suffer, wasn't it?"

Colin collapsed into the chair across from her bed with a weariness that seemed more of the heart than the body. For the first time it struck Sally as strange that they'd never talked about this before.

They'd both supported Beth through every stage of her cancer from the day she'd found the lump, to the day she'd finally died. Two years of their lives, and yet never had she and Colin shared what they were going through.

And since the funeral, they hadn't spoken at all.

Even now, she spoke hesitantly. "This may sound trite, but she was such a genuinely good person. I'd known her since she was a schoolgirl and I never saw her do anything mean to anyone."

"Her students loved her. She got letters from all her second-graders. Those were the letters I found hardest to read after…after she was gone."

"She loved those kids so much." Beth had been a natural with children. That she'd never managed to have one of her own had been her biggest regret. "And she was always so good to Lara."

"What do you miss the most?" Colin asked.

"That's a tough one." There were so many things. The annual holiday they took back to the lake in Saskatchewan where they'd gone to camp when they'd been kids. Their movie dates, where they alternately laughed and cried through the chick-flicks the men in their lives refused to see. The times they'd shared a bottle of wine and just talked.

"You know, I think I missed her the most on my birthday." For the first time in Sally's life, the day had passed unremarked by anyone. Her parents were gone, she had no husband, and Lara, with her father that weekend, had forgotten to phone. "Beth *always* took me out for lunch on my birthday."

"I remember."

Sally shifted into a sitting position. The pain in her head had settled into a moderate throbbing. Her hand, treated with cream and wrapped in a bandage, no longer burned. "What about you? What do you miss most?"

"Her smile, I guess. Or maybe the way she always worried her eyebrows when she was concentrating."

Sally gave a snort. "That was so annoying."

"I know. But sort of cute, too. How about that yellow blouse she wore every Easter?"

"With the embroidered Easter eggs? God, that was so tacky."

"She wore it because the kids loved the colors. Remember how she used to play Neil Diamond when she was in an especially good mood?"

Sally sang the first couple of lines of "Sweet Caroline," with Colin joining in partway through. Eventually they forgot the words and, after they'd both given up on the song, their glances caught and held. Sally felt as if her own grief was being mirrored right back at her.

He really loved Beth, Sally thought. Not that she'd ever doubted it. She'd known her best friend had a great marriage. But he'd *really* loved her.

"Speaking selfishly," Colin said, picking up the thread of conversation, "I'd have to say I miss her companionship when I come home from work—not to mention her cooking. She knew all my favorites."

"And what would those be?"

"Anything with a tomato sauce. Pizza. Lasagna. She made the best chicken cacciatore."

"Same things we ate when we were university roommates." Beth had done most of the cooking then, too, Sally recalled. "So what do you eat for your dinners now?" she asked Colin. "Takeout?"

"No. I boil things. Microwave things. Grill things. I just can't *cook* anything."

"So by cooking, you mean combining more than one ingredient in the same pot?"

"I guess that's what I mean."

"I should teach you how to stir-fry. It's sort of like cooking, only easier. And healthy, too."

"Is that what you were doing tonight when you had your…fall?"

"Yes." Why had he hesitated that way? Sally angled her head for a closer look at him. Two minutes ago Colin had seemed ready to spend the night in that chair. Now he was poised on the edge of the seat cushion, watching her closely.

Did he suspect that there was nothing at all accidental in what had happened to her? For a moment she considered confiding in him. But could she really trust Colin with this when she, herself, didn't know how to react?

Besides, she had to remember that to Colin, Neil was a respected colleague. And a friend, too. After all, they'd gone to school together. And when Sally and Neil had been married, they'd gone out with Colin and Beth occasionally.

Sally's instincts were to keep silent. She had to figure out what had happened and why. She needed to step carefully, because if she made any mistakes, Neil would make her pay, for sure.

And even though they were having a nice conversation tonight, Colin wasn't someone she wanted to take into her confidence. Ever since she'd found out Beth was in love with him, she'd walked on eggshells around the man.

"Is Lara at Neil's?"

"She's at a sleepover party."

"What time are you supposed to pick her up in the morning?"

"She's getting a ride. She'll be home around eleven."

"Right. That's taken care of, then. Where would you like me to sleep?"

Right where you are. Of course, Sally didn't dare say that, even though it was so comforting having him close. "The spare room is down the hall to the left. There are clean towels in the bathroom closet."

"Okay." Colin stood and stretched out his tall, large-boned frame. He cut an imposing figure in the broad-shouldered suits he wore to work, but to Sally's mind he looked even better in the jeans and plain blue T-shirt he wore tonight.

He left the room, and moments later Sally heard him moving around in the kitchen. Was he cleaning up the mess from her aborted stir-fry?

He was back ten minutes later. "Still awake?"

"So far," she agreed.

"You had a lot of food prepared," he commented.

Neil had said the same thing.

"A lot of food for just one person."

Where was he going with that? She made a noise of disgruntlement. "I was alone, okay? I burned myself and I fell. I've always been kind of clumsy."

Colin folded his arms over his chest. In the low light, she couldn't see his eyes at all. "I've always thought of you as graceful, actually."

Really? She felt something lurch inside her, a pleased yet shy reaction that reminded her of her younger self. It had been a long time since a man's compliment had elicited such a response from her.

"I'm going to leave the hall light on, okay? You know I have to wake you up in a few hours to give you another quiz."

"I'll bone up on provincial capitals while I'm sleeping."

Colin smiled. It seemed as if he was going to leave, then he changed his mind and took a couple of steps inside her room.

"Sally, I know you told me you were by yourself when you fell tonight. Are you sure about that? Is there any chance your head injury affected your memory?"

She was so tempted to tell him. But the habit of holding her best friend's husband at a distance was too ingrained to break now.

"I was alone and I fell, Colin. That's all."

He looked at her sadly, as if her answer had disappointed him.

"By the way," he said. "There's a silver pen on your island. It's engraved with the initials 'N.A.'"

The pen she had used to sign the passport application earlier. Trust the crown prosecutor to have noticed that. He was looking at her expectantly now. Waiting for her confession, no doubt. But she wasn't giving in to his courtroom tactics.

"I guess Neil must have left it here the last time he came to visit Lara," she replied softly. Then she closed her eyes and pretended to sleep.

CHAPTER THREE

AT TWO O'CLOCK in the morning, the alarm on Colin's wristwatch began to beep. He'd been sleeping lightly and woke easily. Careful not to disturb Armani at the foot of the bed, he got up and pulled on his jeans.

When the puppy had started whimpering an hour ago, Colin hadn't wanted him to wake Sally, so he'd let him into his room. The puppy had hopped up onto the bed as if permission were a forgone conclusion. Colin suspected this was not the case. Still, at least the dog had been happy.

Colin crept down the hallway. At the entrance to Sally's room, he paused. The door stood open, and light from the hall spilled onto Sally's bed, highlighting the blond streaks in her hair and emphasizing her pale complexion. One hand, the uninjured one, clutched the sheet, holding it to her chin.

She looked unaccustomedly young, vulnerable and sweet. And seeing her that way filled Colin with an uncomfortable guilt.

In the almost twenty years he'd known her, Sally had rarely let down her guard around him. He was used to her alert and wary, her keen mind poised to take advantage of his first sign of weakness.

He didn't know why she'd developed an almost instantaneous animosity toward him. He supposed it had all began in Foundations to Law—their very first class on the first day of law school.

He'd stood up to disagree with a point she was making—about what, he could no longer remember. He'd turned her opinion into a joke and made the entire class laugh. Sally had appeared to take the insult calmly, but from that moment on, she'd made a point of gunning for him whenever she could.

She'd proved herself a worthy adversary, in a battle that Colin soon understood he was destined to lose.

Because it hadn't taken more than a few weeks for him to realize Sally was the last woman he wanted to argue with. But his belated attempts to win her over had failed miserably.

For almost three years they had failed, and then, inexplicably, they hadn't.

It was just a week before December exams, in their final year, when he'd offered Sally a ride home from the library and she'd surprised him by accepting. In the car that night, they had managed to have their first real conversation since they'd met. And when he'd invited her to his off-campus apartment, she'd accepted.

They'd made love that night and their relationship had changed.

Only, unknown to him, the cute education student he'd dated a couple of times previously was Sally's best friend and roommate. Once Sally connected the dots—apparently she'd never in a million years have surmised from Beth's glowing descriptions that her friend was talking about Colin Foster—she'd become colder and more antagonistic than ever.

He'd only just met Beth. He hadn't been in love with her yet. "I'm not going to ask her out again," he'd told Sally when she'd decreed their one night together would never be repeated.

"I still won't get involved with you," Sally swore. And that very night she was on Neil Anderson's arm at the university pub.

Every day for a whole week Colin had fought her to change her mind. Finally, angry at her stubbornness, he *had* asked Beth out again and his relationship with Sally had reverted to its original footings with one twist. They still argued, disagreed and, whenever possible, avoided each other. But underlying the old antagonism was a new awareness that could leave him momentarily breathless in her presence.

To his consternation, Sally had seemed impervious to this new affliction of his, suffering none of the same side effects herself.

She was the strongest woman he'd ever known. Throughout Beth's illness, she'd never broken down. That must be why seeing her hurt and needing his help felt like an invasion of her privacy.

He went to her bedside and flicked on the reading lamp. "Sally? Can you wake up for a minute?"

He put his hand on her shoulder and was surprised how fragile and womanly that one, innocent body part felt. Even covered in flannel. He squeezed, then gave a gentle shake. "Sally?"

"What?" Her good hand let go of the sheet in order to brush the hair off her face. "Colin?"

She sounded startled, but not afraid.

"This can't be true," she murmured, her eyes suddenly open wide and staring at him.

Both pupils equal in size, he noted in the logical side of his brain. His emotional half wished he could fold this woman within his arms and crawl into bed with her. She looked…cuddly. Adorable.

Sally Stowe cuddly and adorable? Impossible.

He could tell the second Sally's full consciousness returned. Her hand touched the sore spot on her head and her eyes gained their usual sharp focus.

"There are ten provinces in Canada, fifty states in America, and the Flames are in the running for the Stanley Cup this year. Can I go back to sleep, please?"

It was a relief to know she was okay. That she hadn't seriously injured herself with that fall. Still, he wouldn't have minded if the more vulnerable Sally had hung around for a while longer.

"All clear," he said, resisting the impulse to touch her cheek. "Good night, Sally."

She closed her eyes and seemed to fall back to sleep instantly. He paused, inexplicably reluctant to leave her alone in this room.

What if, he started to think. *What if…?*

But he couldn't let himself finish that question, not even in his mind. To wish he might have had a future with Sally meant repudiating his years with Beth. And he could never do that.

EIGHT HOURS AFTER he'd left his ex-wife lying on her kitchen floor, Neil Anderson's conscience began to trouble him. He'd just dropped off the young lawyer he'd taken to dinner. They'd had sex at his place after, but he hadn't wanted her to stay the night. Even though Lara wasn't with him this weekend, that was one of his rules. No women overnight. Ever.

Maybe that was harsh, but it wasn't his fault he had to live his life this way. He didn't want to be with a different woman every month or so, shuffling them out the door when the good times were over. He wanted what every man had the right to expect. His wife in bed with him at night and still there when he woke the next morning.

Sally.

Neil's hands tightened on the steering wheel. Full of resentment, he turned toward the Elbow Valley community.

He hadn't meant to hurt her tonight, of course. He still couldn't believe he'd actually shoved her that hard. That was all it had been, though—a shove. It wasn't his fault she'd been stupid enough to touch the stove, or that her head had knocked against the stone counter. When he'd left her she was conscious. He was sure he'd heard her moan.

But in the past hour he'd started to worry. What if she'd been injured more seriously than he thought? You could never tell with trauma to the head. Since Lara was out for the night, Sally could end up lying on the floor until morning.

But as he turned onto her street, he saw that she wasn't alone. There was an SUV he didn't recognize parked in her driveway. What the hell was going on? He glanced at his dash. It was almost three in the morning. The lights were out in the house, so Sally wasn't entertaining late.

Unless this was a party for two.

Neil pulled up next to the SUV. He got out of his car and touched the hood of the other vehicle. Stone cold.

He turned to the house, went to the window and peered inside. Couldn't see anything except a faint light from the hall that led to the bedrooms.

Was Sally scared to sleep in the dark?

Or maybe she wasn't sleeping.

He didn't like the thought of that. Not one bit.

He considered sneaking inside—he'd made a copy of Lara's house key shortly after they'd moved into the new place and Lara had told him the security code, too. But there was the dog to contend with. Before they'd bought that miserable animal, he'd indulged in the occasional late-night foray. Those days were over now. He couldn't take the chance that the dog would bark.

Neil shoved his hands into his pockets, frustrated.

He was a family man. This house should be *theirs* not *hers* and he should be in bed with her right now, their three kids sleeping down the hall.

Instead, Sally lived on her own and he only saw his daughter on alternate weekends and every Wednesday.

Neil's fingers closed around the key in his pocket. He rubbed it as if it was a charm, wishing he could somehow transport himself inside without the dog noticing. He was desperate to find out if Sally was sleeping with the guy who belonged to this SUV.

If she was, it was a big deal. Sally didn't hook up with many men. He'd made it his business to keep tabs on her life, especially her love life. It was not only his right, as the only man who had ever been married to her, it was his responsibility. They had a daughter after all.

Lara. She was the proof that he and Sally belonged together. How could they not, when the combination of their genes had created someone so wonderful, so perfect.

Neil never stopped marveling over her. Their child was beautiful, smart and kind, and on top of all that, a talented athlete. With Olympic potential. *Olympic.*

You'd think Sally would count her blessings to have a daughter like that. But no, she continued to work—had done so since Lara was eight months old. And not only had she spurned her traditional role as a mother, she'd washed her hands of being a wife, too.

She'd tried to marginalize him. Him, the father of her child. It was a crime. And the bigger sin was this country's liberal legal system that made it possible for women to get away with behavior like that.

Neil cast one more fruitless glance into the house, then finally gave up and headed for his car. Whatever was going on, at least he knew she wasn't unconscious on the kitchen floor. Though now he almost wished she were.

"STILL TIRED after your sleepover?" Sally asked her daughter on Monday morning.

Lara said, "Not really," and then she yawned, which made both of them laugh. "Maybe a little," she conceded.

The weekend, like all of her daughter's weekends, had been busy. After the sleepover, Lara spent Saturday afternoon training with her ski team. On Sunday Sally had driven Lara and her friend Jessica to the ski hill at Sunshine for what would probably be their last ski outing of the season.

Sally had sipped hot chocolate in the lodge while the girls skied like mad all morning. By mid-afternoon the snow turned slushy. They'd left early, dropped Jess at home then had cheese fondue for dinner, followed by a hot bath and bed.

Now, as Lara ate her breakfast, Sally slathered cream cheese on bagels for both of their lunches and cut up fruit.

She worked awkwardly, favoring her left hand. The bandages were off, the exposed skin puckered and tender. But at least the stitches on her head were healing nicely and the headache had cleared. She felt almost normal again, and in the sunlight, with her daughter slouched on a stool at the kitchen counter, and the prospect of a regular workweek ahead of her, it was tempting to chalk up her experience with Neil on Friday as a very bizarre, frightening anomaly.

Neil hadn't meant to hurt her. That wasn't his style. It wouldn't happen again.

But Sally, who specialized in family law, and had volunteered for many years with the Women's Emergency Shelter, had worked around abused women too long to let herself get away with such easy rationalizations.

Neil had crossed a line on Friday night. It was certainly possible he would do it again if the right opportunity presented itself.

She would have to make sure that opportunity never occurred. She wasn't naive or unempowered like so many of her clients. She could handle this situation. She could handle Neil. Later she would phone a handyman service to get the kitchen door fixed so it would be easier to keep locked. She'd make better use of her alarm system, too.

Those were both good, concrete steps to take, but Sally was afraid they wouldn't be enough. The real problem here was that Neil was Lara's father, and as such, Sally couldn't barricade him from her house or her life as thoroughly as she wanted.

Had she made a mistake not reporting his assault to the police?

She knew what her answer would have been for a client in a similar situation. Definitely, she should have contacted the police, if only to have a record of her complaint.

She knew it, but she still couldn't make herself take such a drastic step. Accusing Neil would set an unavoidable sequence of events into motion. For sure Neil would deny the charges. The ensuing battle would be horrible for Lara. Friends and associates would find themselves choosing sides. Many, she feared, would refuse to believe that Neil was capable of such behavior.

The scandal would probably wreck her chances of becoming a judge, at least this time around. And who knew when the next opportunity would arise?

Sally packed Lara's bagel and fruit into a bag, along with a yogurt and a couple of cookies. "I guess we'd better get moving. You can finish your toast in the car."

Lara slid to the floor. Her tight jeans and T-shirt revealed the subtle new curves to her lean, athletic body.

My baby, Sally thought, sadly. Why did she have to grow up so fast?

"I have to go to Jessica's to work on our social studies project after school," Lara reminded her, as she shifted her backpack onto her shoulders. "Can you pick me up at six?"

"No problem." Sally tossed her own lunch into her briefcase then slipped on her blazer and made sure her cell phone was clipped at her waist. She let Armani inside and put him in the laundry room with his toys and water. She'd hired a pet-sitting service to come into the house around noon to take him for a walk. Still, she piled newspapers in the corner of the room in case he had an accident.

Lara stopped to give him a hug on her way out the door. "I love you, Armani."

Following their morning routine, Sally dropped her daughter off at school, then headed for her downtown office. During this part of the drive she usually turned off the radio station her daughter liked to listen to and focused on the day ahead of her.

But today she couldn't concentrate on her morning appointments.

Colin Foster. She'd done her best not to think of him since he'd left her house on Saturday morning, about half an hour before Lara was scheduled to come home. She didn't want to remember how unexpectedly kind and gentle he'd been with her.

Oh, she'd seen him that way with Beth, especially in the later stages of the cancer. But Sally had never expected to experience such treatment herself.

Or to enjoy it so much.

Poor Colin must have had very little sleep on Friday night. He'd checked on her several times, and once she'd woken to see him sprawled out in the chair in her room. Their glances had connected across the quiet bedroom, then she'd pretended to fall back asleep again.

In the morning he'd made her breakfast. Boiled eggs and coffee and lightly browned toast. They'd shared the weekend paper, reading out snippets of interesting facts to each other.

He'd fussed over her a little, but not too much.

She couldn't remember the last time someone had taken care of her that way. Probably her Mom when Sally had the chicken pox in grade six.

Don't be so nice to me, she'd longed to say to him. Colin Foster was easy to handle when he was acting arrogant and overconfident. This other side of him put her off balance.

Determinedly, Sally blocked the mental image of Colin at her breakfast table from her mind. Her life was complicated enough without her searching for more things to worry about.

With a sigh, she turned the radio back on, and was accosted by a mechanical beat and repetitive rap lyrics. Heavens, why did Lara like this stuff?

SALLY'S FIRST APPOINTMENT of the day was with Pamela Moore, a woman in her early thirties who was having problems with her ex-husband, Rick. According to the terms of their divorce settlement, Rick was supposed to pay just over eight hundred dollars a month in child support. He hadn't done so for the past four months.

As she sipped her first coffee of the day, Sally thumbed through the Moore's thick file. Ninety-nine percent of her clients were just that—people she was hired to represent. But Pam was different.

She'd first become aware of Pam's difficult situation when she'd been volunteering her legal services at the Women's Emergency Shelter. Pam had shown up with bruises distorting her facial features, but it didn't take long for the two women to realize they knew each other.

They'd both grown up in Medicine Hat, a medium-size city about three hours southeast of Calgary. Pam's family had been regulars at Sally's parents' café. On a couple of occasions, Sally had babysat for Pam and her two younger brothers.

So Pam wasn't just a client, and while Sally fought hard for all her clients, for Pam she pulled out all the stops. She wanted the younger woman and her two children to have a future far better than what they'd experienced so far.

But Pam's ex-husband seemed equally determined not to let that happen. He'd battled Pam on every step of her attempt to leave him and regain control of her life. Most inexcusable to Sally, throughout the entire struggle, he'd shown little interest in their children. And even less interest in contributing toward their financial support.

Rick's main goal was winning Pam back. Twice he'd convinced her to try a reconciliation. On both occasions, Pam had ended up at the shelter with a few more bruises and an even more battered self-esteem.

Sally asked her why she kept giving him more chances.

"He's the father of my children. And you don't know the pressure he's under. He runs his own business. He has to work so hard."

Sometimes Sally was tempted to say, "I'm a businesswoman, too. I'm under a lot of pressure. But it would never occur to me to beat someone up because of it." Of course, she never actually said this. Pam was smart enough to understand it wasn't so much Sally, as herself, that she was trying to convince.

Eventually a late-night visit to Emergency to treat her broken arm had convinced Pamela to leave Rick for good. The divorce had been ugly. Despite a restraining order against him, Rick still found ways to inject misery into Pamela's life.

Sally had just reviewed the last of the documentation in the file, when Evelyn at the front desk gave her a buzz.

"Pamela Moore to see you, Ms. Stowe."

"Thanks. Tell her I'll be right there."

Though one of the younger partners at the firm, Sally had a coveted outer office with a mountain view. Early in her career she'd caught the attention of senior partner Gerald Thornton. "I like the way you think," he'd told her. "More than that, I like the way you never give up."

Gerald's opinions carried a lot of weight, not only in the firm, but also in the legal community at large. It was through his connections that she'd wound up president of the Law Society of Alberta, a position that had enabled her to meet many of the province's most influential high fliers.

Gerald was also behind the current push to get her into the Court of Queen's Bench. As she passed by his big corner office, Sally remembered he was out of town on business this week. He'd asked her to cover in court for him later this afternoon.

In the reception area she found Pam perched on the edge of a chair, flipping through *People*. She tossed the magazine to the table and jumped to her feet when she saw Sally.

"I'm on a break," she said. "I only have fifteen minutes."

Sally had pulled strings to get Pam an office job at the courthouse, which unfortunately didn't pay that much, but it was a start. Since black jeans were the dressiest item in Pam's closet, she'd also given the young mother some suits she rarely wore and money for tailoring. Pam was wearing the green linen today.

"You look good, Pam."

"I feel good. If only Rick—"

"I know. Come on, let's talk." Sally put a hand on her arm and ushered Pam to her office. When Pam was seated and the door closed, she quickly turned to business.

"What is Rick up to this time?" The fact that

Rick owned his own business had made collecting child support a challenge from the beginning. They couldn't request that his employer deduct the money straight from his salary, because he had no employer. Then he'd tried some accounting tricks—officially reducing his salary to a nominal amount while allowing funds to accumulate in the business.

Pam had gone to Maintenance Enforcement for help and they'd put a hold on his driving privileges in order to force him to meet his responsibilities to his children.

And now—

"The bastard sold his business. Just to spite me, I'm sure."

"But how is he supporting himself?" Rick rented a posh condo in trendy downtown Eau Claire. And he had an extravagant lifestyle to go with it.

"He let the apartment go and moved in with his mother."

"You're kidding!"

"He says there's no sense working when half his money goes to taxes and the rest to me."

"As if. What is wrong with the man? He's cramping his own lifestyle as well as yours."

"When it comes to hurting me, Rick has always been willing to go that extra mile."

"Surely he won't keep this up for long. A man like

Rick can't be happy living with his mother. Not working."

"He's taking computer classes at SAIT. Claims he wants to open a new computer service business when he's done. I can't afford to wait him out, Sally. I'm behind on my own rent now. I could barely scrape together the money for Tabby's antibiotics when she got an ear infection last week. I've asked my parents for help—again—but I can't keep putting them in this situation."

"I hear you, Pam." But if Rick wasn't working, he had no income. "What did he do with the proceeds of his business?"

"He wouldn't tell me, but a mutual friend says he bought some land down by Pincher Creek. He isn't renting it or anything, so there's no income from that source, either."

Land. Sally smiled. "We can register a support order against his property to create a lien."

"What does that mean?"

"You need to contact Maintenance Enforcement again. They'll file a writ against the land on your behalf. Unfortunately, that won't put any cash in your pocket right now, but when he goes to sell—which he'll undoubtedly want to do soon—he'll have to pay you arrears plus interest."

"Sally, I need money now. Or the kids and I are going to have to go back to the shelter."

"Phone Maintenance Enforcement today. Hopefully just the threat of action will get Rick to pay. Besides, how much longer do you think he'll be able to stand living with his mother?" Pam had told her before how the woman drove both her and Rick crazy with her nosy interference.

"I guess it's worth a try." Pamela glanced at her watch. "I should be getting back to work. The last thing I need right now is to lose my job."

"Okay. Try not to worry. Rick's not going to get away with this." As Sally walked Pam to the elevators, she asked about the kids. Samuel was now five, Tabby three. Like most mothers, Pam's face lit up as she talked about her children. She was smiling when they parted.

Back in her office, Sally found it more difficult to keep up her own good spirits. She was so tired of dealing with men like Rick. Didn't he see that by lashing out at his former spouse he was hurting his own children?

If only he could be in the position of holding a crying child at night and not having the money to buy the medicine to make her better.

Or would he even care?

Weary already, though it was only ten o'clock, Sally picked up her pen and began to jot notes for the file. The phone rang before she was through the first sentence.

"Sally Stowe speaking."

"Hi, Sal. Hard at work already, are you?"

It was Neil. Sally dropped her pen and ran her hand through her hair until she'd found the neat line of stitches at the side of her head. She traced the line back and forth with her index finger and contemplated hanging up without another word.

"How's Lara?" he asked.

No mention of what had happened Friday night. She'd been half expecting an apology but wasn't surprised he chose not to bring up the incident at all. Maybe he was embarrassed. She hoped so. "Lara's fine. Gearing up for the big race next weekend."

"I'll be taking her to that," he said.

It was Neil's weekend with Lara coming up. "I know." If she and Neil were able to get along better, she would have loved to watch the races, too. But Lara became anxious whenever she and Neil were in close proximity.

"Lara needs to be in top condition for the weekend," Neil warned. "Feed her lots of meat—a good steak dinner or a roast beef. Not just those god-awful tofu stir-fries you like to eat."

"I'll make sure Lara has plenty of protein." Sally rolled her eyes, though in truth she was comfortable with this, the negotiating of care for their daughter. She didn't really mind Neil checking up on her this

way, even though his concern was totally unneces-
sary. She was thankful that Neil was a good father.
She could put up with his crap as long as he treated
Lara right.

"And don't let her stay up too late at night. She
needs to be rested."

"Of course." Lord, Neil could be so overbearing.

Suddenly his voice switched from a lecturing tone
to something soft and intimate. "Oh, and Sal?"

On guard, she said cautiously, "Yes?"

"How's the new boyfriend?"

"What?" He'd caught her completely by surprise
with this one.

"Don't play innocent. I saw the SUV in your
driveway on Saturday morning. It was still there
until just before Lara got home."

Neil had seen Colin's vehicle? Sally felt suddenly
ill to her stomach. How long had he been watching
her house? Was this something he did often?

"This is none of your business, Neil."

"Maybe not. Still, you ought to be careful. A
judge has to be circumspect about the men she's
keeping company with. Especially a judge who
hasn't yet been officially appointed."

The bastard was trying to threaten her. She remembered the last words he'd uttered on Friday
night before he'd left her half-unconscious on the
kitchen floor. He'd said he would make sure she was

never appointed to the bench. He'd promised to see her disbarred instead.

Sally hung up the phone firmly. She wouldn't let her ex play these mind games with her. He might be a very successful criminal lawyer with political connections of his own, but he couldn't touch her. She'd done nothing wrong.

Even as she had that thought, she pictured Colin Foster reclined on the chair in her bedroom, watching her with a light in his eyes that she recognized all too well.

Had he realized how much she'd wanted to invite him into her bed with her?

Oh, Lord. How could she feel this way about the man who had been her best friend's husband?

CHAPTER FOUR

SINCE BETH'S DEATH, Colin had started getting to work late. This was a direct corollary to his sleeping pattern, which involved tossing restlessly in bed until about four or five in the morning, at which time he would finally drop off, only to be awoken by his alarm a few hours later.

Inevitably, he hit the snooze button. Once, twice, a third time.

There was no warm body beside him to kick his shin. No cranky voice to say, "If you hit that thing one more time…"

As a teacher, Beth's workday had started an hour later than his. A good thing, since she'd never been a morning person, while Colin loved the peace and quiet of dawn, the opportunity to savor the beginning of a day filled with possibilities. In an ideal world, he was the first to arrive at the office. He'd turn on the photocopier, start a pot of coffee, then sequester himself in his office to review the list of cases he would be prosecuting that day.

This Monday morning, however, was turning out far from ideal. After too many jabs of the snooze button, he rushed into the office only thirty minutes before he needed to be in court. Aware that his jacket was improperly buttoned and his jaw still bled from a rush job of shaving, he tried to hurry into the sanctuary of his office.

"Good morning, Mr. Foster." The front-desk receptionist eyed him with an indulgent, if slightly worried, smile.

He ducked his head and aimed for the main corridor where he almost bowled over a prosecutor he'd worked with for years.

"Hi, Colin. Any chance you can make lunch tomorrow?"

"I'll get back to you on that." He nodded and picked up his pace. Only a couple more steps and he would be—

The articling student he'd hired last summer materialized in front of him. "I have a question about that file you left on my desk yesterday."

He held up a hand, in a gesture that meant *later,* and finally slipped gratefully into his office. He closed the door, sighed then turned around.

Only to see one of the junior prosecutors waiting by the window. Judith Daigle had entered the law profession late, after a messy divorce at age thirty-three. She was now thirty-eight, a member of the bar and, since Beth's death, unremittingly attentive.

"Good morning, Colin. Did you have a good weekend? I hope you enjoyed the casserole."

Colin didn't have the heart to tell her the truth—that he'd tossed it, and the aluminum pan it came in, straight into the garbage. Once, when he'd stopped by Judith's house to drop off a writ, he'd seen a fat orange tabby—one of several of Judith's cats—parading on her kitchen table. With that picture in his mind, he couldn't bring himself to eat any of the meals she so thoughtfully prepared for him.

He wished he could think of some polite way to make her stop cooking for him.

"How was your weekend, Judith?" He slid behind his desk, aligned the buttons on his jacket, then tapped on his keyboard. Sixty-five unread messages in his e-mail in-box. God only knows how many he'd find in voice mail.

"My weekend was quiet." Judith always gave the same answer when he asked that question.

Colin suspected she was looking to him to change the situation. As with the casseroles, he wished he could think of some polite way to make her stop.

"I thought you might want to review the Mueller case. As you suspected, he does have a record of similar offenses."

"Is the record in his file?" Colin opened the top one in a pile on his desk.

"Yes, I—"

"That should be all I need, then." He slipped on the reading glasses he had only just begun to need and focused on the papers in front of him, barely registering the moment when Judith left the room.

I should have said thanks, at least. He felt guilty about that. But then, Judith had a way of making him feel guilty about a lot of things.

If it wasn't for the cats, maybe things could have been different. She owned so many. He'd counted five on that one visit. Judith was attractive. Intelligent. Obviously available. She had nice legs, too.

Not as nice as Sally's, but then Sally was a bit of a phenomenon in that area.

He'd wondered how far he would get into his day before he thought of her. But this wasn't even the first time. Visions of her had been in his head when he woke up this morning. And she'd come to mind a couple times during the drive to work, as well.

She wasn't telling him the truth about Friday night. He knew that for sure. He could have bought a burned hand. But a fall against the granite counter, too? No way. Not unless she'd had a seizure of some sort.

He drew a question mark on the pad of paper by his phone. Could that be it? Was Sally ill?

He hated that possibility. But it was an option he had to consider, although Neil's pen on the otherwise spotless counter suggested a second scenario. Perhaps Sally and her ex had argued. Then what? Colin knew their divorce had been far from amicable, but he couldn't picture the sophisticated and courteous Neil resorting to physical violence.

Had someone else been in the house, then? After Neil left? One of Sally's client's disgruntled husbands?

The buzzer on the phone intercom sounded, cutting into his conjectures. "Mr. Foster? It's time for you to go to court."

Hell. He hadn't even finished reviewing the files. Colin gathered them into a stack, then shoved them into his briefcase, promising himself he'd follow up on Sally's "accident" later.

DURING THE DRIVE HOME, Colin's speculations focused on the possibility that Sally might have suffered a seizure of some sort. But if so, why not admit the truth to him? Was she worried that if news of her illness became known, it might get in the way of her judicial aspirations?

He'd heard the scuttlebutt and knew she was a favored contender for Justice Willa Kendal's position on the Queen's Bench. Willa had been diagnosed with Parkinson's a few months ago and was officially retiring at the beginning of June.

Her replacement would be announced shortly after that date and Sally was high on the committee's list of potential candidates for several reasons. First, she was a woman, and given the current composition of the courts, that was an important factor. Although she was young, Sally had had a distinguished career. Her integrity was unquestioned. Her politics fortuitously aligned with the current reigning powers.

Colin pulled into his garage, surprised to find himself home already. His stomach felt a little off, and it only took a minute for him to realize why.

I don't want Sally to be sick.

She didn't look unwell, but then neither had Beth, at least not in the beginning.

Colin was suddenly so weary he could hardly get out of his vehicle. As his gaze skimmed by the Miata, his conscience pricked. He'd promised himself he was going to start doing the things that needed to be done.

And he would. But later.

In the house, he went straight to the kitchen, to the fridge, to the line of aluminum cans that filled the space that had once contained real food like milk and juice and carefully labeled Tupperware containers of leftovers.

He snagged a beer, was about to close the fridge door, when he noticed the plastic container behind the dozen ale. He'd seen it a hundred times before, and done his best to ignore it, but this time he made the effort to reach deep into the cold cavern and pull it out.

Low-fat cherry yogurt. Beth's favorite kind.

The container felt heavy. Through the opaque white plastic, he imagined he could see the green froth of mold. Holding the container at arm's length, he carried it to the trash, then let it drop.

It fell right on top of the aluminum pan containing Judith's casserole.

ON TUESDAY SALLY MET Justice Kendal for lunch at a small bistro down from the courthouse. The judge was sixty-eight, unmarried, sharp of mind and tongue. She carried her short, rotund body with authority, and stress lines marred a face that would still be considered pretty if not for her stern visage.

Even though they'd been on a first-name basis for years, Sally always felt a little intimidated in her presence, as though Willa were somehow a species above the rest of humanity.

As Willa lifted her fork to her mouth, though, her hand betrayed her all too mortal origins. While Sally had noticed the tremors for almost a year, they'd only recently been diagnosed as Parkinson's disease.

"I hope you've been whittling down your client

load, as I've advised you." Willa spoke with her usual authority, as if completely unfazed by the fact that she could barely feed herself.

Sally would have liked to lean over the table and offer a steady hand. But she knew Willa would prefer if she pretended nothing was wrong. So she did not offer to help, instead forking a strand of pasta into her own mouth.

As she did so, Willa's attention went to the discolored skin on Sally's hand. Sally waited for her to ask what had happened.

I burned myself cooking on the weekend. That was what she'd told everyone else who'd inquired. And each time, she thought to herself, *I'm going to have to do something about Neil.* But so far, she'd taken no action. She hadn't even had her door fixed, though she was more careful about keeping it locked.

But Willa didn't ask about her hand. "Well? Are you making all the appropriate arrangements?"

Sally pushed the remaining pasta to a corner of her plate. "I'm working on it."

"When you get the call from the justice minister, you are no longer allowed to work as an attorney."

When you get the call. Not *if.* Willa had so much confidence in her. Sally hoped it was justified. And she had been doing her best to sort out her clients in the event that she was lucky enough to get the appointment. She'd spoken to a couple of her fellow lawyers about sharing the load.

But some clients were harder to hand over than others. Pamela Moore, for instance. She was more of a friend than a client. Though it went against her usual office policy of requiring an up-front retainer, Sally had never sent the woman a single bill. Who was going to take on a client like that?

Willa reached across the table to pat her hand. "You're an excellent attorney, Sally, but not the only excellent attorney in the city."

Sally allowed a smile. "I suppose that's true." She stared out the window and saw fresh raindrops splatter on the sidewalks and streets. The dreary spring weather matched her mood today.

"I just wish it wasn't happening this way." She hated knowing that her judicial appointment, the highlight of her career, was only possible because Willa Kendal had a chronic, eventually fatal, condition.

"Don't get maudlin, Sally. I can't handle that sort of thing. If it wasn't my retirement, it would be someone else's."

In Canada, where judges were appointed for life, not elected, openings occurred under two circumstances only—the retirement or the death of an existing judge.

"This is your chance. You've earned it."

"Thanks, Willa. You've been such a supportive friend to me." Willa had hired her out of law school. Sally had articled at Willa's firm, then later, when Willa had been appointed to the bench, she had introduced Sally to Gerald Thornton, who had brought her in as a junior partner at Crane, Whyte and Thornton.

"You think you don't give as good as you get?" Willa abandoned her efforts to eat and downed the rest of her cola. Since court was in session this afternoon, she wasn't drinking wine, her preferred luncheon beverage. "Now, tell me about that girl of yours. Is she still skiing competitively?"

Sally nodded. "The last race of the season is this weekend."

"She's pretty serious?"

Again Sally nodded. "Her coach seems to think she has Olympic potential."

"You have mixed feelings about that?"

Sally wasn't surprised at her friend's perceptiveness. You didn't get to be a judge without developing the ability to read people accurately. Once again, Willa was on the mark.

"I can't help but wonder if Olympic-level skiing—with all the pressure, demands and risk of injury—is the right course for Lara. She says, yes, but she's only sixteen. Is that really old enough to be making such an important decision?"

"What does that charming ex-husband of yours think?"

Sally tried not to resent Willa speaking of Neil in such positive terms. She reminded herself that Neil did seem to hold a special appeal for older women. And Willa knew nothing about the reasons for their divorce. Sally had never taken her into her confidence on that particular subject.

"He's thrilled. He wasn't much of an athlete when he was younger. I think he's living vicariously through our daughter."

"I guess he wouldn't be the first father to do that. And how does he feel about the possibility of you becoming a Justice of the Queen's Bench?"

Sally tilted her water glass and watched the ice cubes bob accordingly. "It's hard to say."

"We had lunch last week. I thought he seemed very proud of you."

Willa and Neil had lunched together? That explained where Neil had learned about her application. The sneaky bastard. "I didn't realize you and Neil were friends."

"Why Sally. You aren't jealous?" Willa winked, then laughed. "Actually, it was just one of those coincidences. I was lunching on my own, and he happened to walk into the restaurant at just the right moment."

Sally tried not to feel suspicious. It could have happened the way Willa had described. Just one of those serendipitous meetings. Yet, knowing Neil, she doubted it.

"Neil is right to be proud of you, Sally. You're still so young. Your future is limitless."

"Thank you, Willa. That's very generous of you to say." Especially in light of Willa's own.

"I daresay Neil's success will match yours. His reputation in criminal law is becoming quite formidable."

Sally nodded. Neil had made partner a year before her, and she knew he earned a salary that exceeded her own by at least three times. Those things mattered to him. Not the money, but the prestige factor. In fact, Sally was convinced that his concern about appearances—and not any real worry about Lara's welfare—had been behind his push to get her to be a stay-at-home mom.

For a moment Sally considered telling Willa about Neil's behavior and ensuing threat on Friday night. She longed to confide in someone. In the past that someone might have been Beth.

Now that her best friend was gone, she needed a new confidant. But as she opened her mouth to blurt out her secret, Sally knew Willa was not the right friend for this. Their relationship had always been constructed around careful borders. Besides, Willa liked Neil. She probably wouldn't believe he was capable of the things that he'd done.

So, instead of talking, she put another forkful of pasta into her mouth.

Willa watched her with careful, knowing eyes, as if guessing that Sally had been on the verge of spilling something big. After their meal was over and the check had been split, Willa had some parting words of advice.

"Be careful, Sally. Your behavior these next few months must be absolutely circumspect."

As if Sally didn't know that. Unfortunately, so did Neil.

WEDNESDAY NIGHTS, Sally always worked late, since that was Neil's evening with Lara. This Wednesday she left the office shortly after seven, anticipating mulling over her day during the thirty-minute drive home. Instead, she found herself thinking of last weekend. She still hadn't thanked Colin for coming to her rescue that night. She should have sent him flowers, or maybe a plant for his office. At least a note.

After she turned off the highway into the Elbow Valley community, she stopped her car at the next intersection, a four-way stop. Home was left. To the right was Colin.

In the distance, the jagged profile of the Rocky Mountains stood out against the deep blue of the evening sky. She sat there admiring the view until she saw an approaching vehicle in her rearview mirror. Decision time.

She swung the wheels to the right. This was a route she'd taken countless times in the past, but not once since Beth's funeral. The next time she stopped her car, she was in front of the gracious rundle-rock facade of the Fosters' two-story house. All the lights were off, except for those in one room to the left of the entrance.

Colin's study. Sally remembered the room well. The built-in bookshelves, the desk, leather chair and sofa. The day the big-screen TV had been delivered, Beth had complained—in that fond, slightly exasperated tone that women used when they were talking about a husband they loved—that Colin was going to live in the room now.

Sally and Beth had been in the kitchen, on that day, leaving Colin to deal with the setup of the complicated sound system. Sally had been cutting veggies for a salad, while Beth stirred something on the stove.

Closing her eyes, Sally conjured the memory of her old friend. Beth's smooth, honey-colored hair had been tucked behind her ears and she'd been wearing the pearl-drop earrings Colin had given her on their fifth wedding anniversary.

The details came to Sally so vividly that for a moment she almost believed the past six months had been nothing but an extended nightmare. Beth couldn't really be dead. If Sally got out of the car and rang the doorbell, her friend would be the one to open the door.

She'd pull Sally over the threshold and offer her something to eat. Beth was always trying to feed her, convinced that she worked too hard and skipped lunch too frequently.

Beth. Oh, Beth. Always worried about everyone but herself.

Even when she'd been dying, she'd been concerned about Sally. "Promise me you won't deal with this by spending yet more hours at the office. You need to go out, Sally. Meet new people and make new friends."

Wise advice. But Sally didn't want new friends. She just wanted her old one back.

Sally reached for the tissues she kept in a compartment on the dash. After wiping away the tears, she checked the time. Seven fifty-five. She'd been sitting here for almost half-an-hour.

What was wrong with her?

She took a deep breath, then moved to put the car into Drive. But at that moment, the front door of Beth's house opened and Colin stepped outside.

She felt a moment of panic as he waved at her. What excuse could she give him for showing up this way? Did he know how long she'd been parked in front of his home?

CHAPTER FIVE

SALLY'S FIRST INSTINCT was to drive away. But Colin was already walking toward her car. He had on jeans and an old—a very old—University of Alberta sweatshirt. She'd probably seen him in that sweatshirt a hundred times.

Including, if memory served her correctly, that one, fateful night over sixteen years ago.

When Colin was close enough to touch her car, she lowered the passenger-side window.

For a moment they just looked at each other, and in his eyes she recognized the sorrow that she'd been feeling. She also saw that he was concerned about her. But there was something else present she couldn't name. It was like a spark, alive and glowing. And it reminded her that despite how she felt at times, she was a woman with half her life still in front of her.

Colin walked around her vehicle, then opened the driver-side door. He didn't ask her what she was doing there, just held out his hand.

"Come in for a minute."

It wasn't a question. Sally, who had developed an aversion to men who tried to tell her what to do, held back.

"Please?"

Sally checked the clock again. She had at least an hour before Neil would bring Lara home. The dog-sitter would have taken Armani for a run just two hours ago.

"Okay." She stepped out to the sidewalk, not needing the hand he'd offered.

"Got the keys?" he asked, before locking and closing the door.

He was barefoot, she was surprised to see. "Aren't you cold?" The breeze from the mountains was icy enough for snow. She pulled her trench coat tight to her body.

"Not particularly." He led the way to his house and she followed. Inside, he took her coat, but when he went to hang it in the closet, she objected.

"Just throw it on the chair," she insisted. *Beth had always thrown it on the chair.* She didn't say that last bit aloud, but Colin looked at her as if he knew exactly what she was thinking.

He tossed her coat where she'd asked, then invited her to his study.

Though she'd seen the room many times, Sally had never actually been inside it. She and Beth had always hung out in the kitchen and adjoining family room.

But the study was a nice place, too. The walls, those not covered in bookshelves, were a warm terracotta. The furniture was an inviting dark brown leather that felt soft and soothing to the touch.

He had a minibar in here, with a small sink and fridge.

"Wine?" he asked, and at her nod, he opened a bottle that Sally recognized as one of Beth's favorites. It was probably left over from the case Beth had bought the last time they'd gone to the wine store together. Not long before Beth had been confined to bed.

After passing her a full glass, Colin sat in the big armchair that was clearly his favorite. It had a blanket thrown over one arm and a nearby footstool that Sally could reach from the sofa, too. She watched him place his bare feet up there, and though the room was only dimly lit, she was struck by how extremely long and narrow his feet were.

"Lara has narrow feet, too," she commented inanely.

"Poor kid. Makes it hell to find shoes."

She took a swallow of wine and forced her attention to his face. "I never thanked you for everything you did for me on Friday night."

She should have brought a bottle of wine with her, she realized belatedly.

"That's no problem. I never thanked you either."

"Why would you need to do that?"

"Because of all you did for Beth."

Sally closed her eyes, suddenly grateful he'd chosen to bring her to this room, where her friend's presence was not so powerful. "You don't need to thank me for that. She was my best friend."

Was. *Was.* Sally wondered when, if ever, she would be able to truly accept that. Having seen Beth die before her very eyes ought to have been enough. But the emotional side of Sally's brain seemed to be waiting for something else.

Sally took a sip of the wine, grateful for Colin's silence. Light jazz played softly in the background. The *Larry King Show* was on TV, though the sound had been muted. It was cozy in this room, Sally decided, tucking her feet under her legs, making herself comfortable.

Colin had reclined fully into his chair, tipping his head back and closing his eyes.

It was almost like being alone. And yet—better.

"Sometimes I feel angry at her," Sally found herself confiding. "This isn't how things were supposed to work out. We used to talk about growing old together. Beth was going to teach me how to set my hair in those tight little rollers, and I was going to teach *her* to play bridge. We were both planning to sign up for lawn bowling...."

She almost laughed, remembering the conversations they'd had about never, never getting too old to remember to pluck the long black hairs from each other's chins.

But instead of laughing, a sob escaped from someplace deep in her heart. She put a hand to her mouth. "Sorry."

Colin must have had his own plans about growing old with his wife. But all he said was, "Did you two really talk about stuff like that?"

"Sure."

He processed that for a moment. "Well, I'll lawn bowl and play bridge with you if you want, but the hair rollers are out."

She did laugh that time, couldn't help herself. And after the first couple of seconds, didn't want to help herself. She pictured Colin in white trousers and a knitted vest, his hair white, his hands gnarled and wielding a lawn bowling ball.

In her imagination, she stood beside him, her gray hair, in rollers, hidden beneath a colorful scarf. They'd be arguing, of course, about whatever people argued about when they were lawn bowling.

Sally clutched her middle, suddenly afraid she was going to spill her wine, she was laughing so hard. Colin took the glass from her hand, smiling in a slightly confused way, clearly glad she was amusing herself, though a bit perplexed as to why.

Finally, the giggling spasm passed. Sally shook her head. "I don't know what came over me."

"Don't apologize. I think you needed that—whatever it was." He handed her back her glass.

Yes. Laughter was a great way to release tension. Of course, so was sex.

Sally gulped more wine. Now that had been a crazy thought. Not to mention, totally inappropriate. What was wrong with her tonight? It couldn't be the wine. She'd barely finished half a glass.

She glanced up at the TV, where Larry King's mouth moved soundlessly. She didn't recognize his guest, but the woman was very young, pretty and blond so she was probably an actress or a model or something. Sally turned back to Colin and found him watching not the TV, but her.

"When was the last time you and I had an argument?" he asked.

"I'm not sure. Last week?" she joked. But actually, she couldn't remember when they'd last disagreed, let alone argued. When Beth had been sick, they'd both decided that whatever Beth wanted, Beth would get. And they'd seen eye-to-eye on what Beth would have preferred in terms of a funeral.

And before Beth had found the lump, she and Colin had seen each other so rarely, really, considering how much time she had spent in his wife's company. Whenever she visited, she'd usually wave at him from the hall and that was it.

"I guess it would be the Wright case," she concluded. That was the last time she'd faced Colin in the courtroom. He'd been prosecuting her client with undue rigor, she'd thought, not taking into consideration the emotional duress Catherine Wright had suffered at the hand of her abusive husband.

Just dredging up the memory, Sally felt some of the buried emotions return to life. "You know he would have killed her if she hadn't stood up to him."

"There are other ways of dealing with a bully besides shooting him in the head, Sally."

On the verge of throwing back a retaliatory argument, Sally found herself suddenly lacking the motivation to do so. They'd covered this ground thoroughly in the courtroom. And ended up with a reasonable compromise, as she recalled.

"We tried the Wright case four years ago," Colin said.

"That long?"

He nodded. He was still watching her. Hadn't taken his eyes off her since she'd entered the room. She realized he was looking at her the way a man looks at a woman when he wants to—

Her body temperature flared with the sudden sexual awareness.

She saw Colin's gaze dip to the swell of her

breasts against the silk fabric of her blouse. He looked at her there, then met her eyes straight on again, communicating desire with no apologies.

She hadn't been sexually active in a long time. As the mother of a young girl, she dated circumspectly. The decision to spend a night with a man was a huge deal to her. Since Neil, there'd only been a couple. And she'd been divorced for almost thirteen years.

Her physical needs were something she'd learned to put to the side. But tonight, suddenly, she felt that age-old hunger. And, obviously Colin felt it, too.

The way he was looking at her…

For an instant, Sally imagined giving in to the feeling, as she once had when they were both students. They'd met at the library and had gotten into an argument about something or other. When the library closed, Colin had offered to drive her home.

Only they hadn't gotten that far, because his apartment had been closer…

"Want a drink?" he'd offered, but it had only been an excuse and she had known it. He'd no sooner closed the apartment door behind them, than they'd kissed as if they'd been starved for the taste of each other.

They'd completely forgotten about whatever point was under debate. Instead, they made love that night, three times, as she recalled. Then in the morning she'd hustled home to shower and change before her first class.

That had been the first and the last time they'd been together. Colin had tried, repeatedly, to get her to go out with him again. But she'd had one very good reason for saying no.

The same reason she had to keep her distance tonight.

"I should be getting home." Sally set down the wineglass on a nearby table.

"If you're sure." He spoke the words reluctantly, and was slow to stand up from his chair. Sally could guess why. It wasn't easy for her, either, to truncate so ruthlessly a moment that could have turned in a completely different direction.

"So…" She lingered in the doorway a moment. "Thanks again for Friday."

"Anytime. I mean that, Sally. If you ever need a hand, just call."

"Thank you," she said again, even though she knew he was the last person she should get used to counting on.

WHAT HAD THAT been all about? Sally felt emotionally exposed, physically sluggish and wanted only to fall into bed and sleep.

But Armani needed to be taken outside, and no sooner had she done that, than Neil returned with their daughter.

She met them at the front door, Armani leashed

and held tightly to her side. Lara looked tired but happy. She held her sports bag in one hand and the remains of a Peter's Drive-In milk shake in the other. While Neil unloaded her skis into the garage, Sally gave her daughter a hug.

It was strange to have to reach up a little to do this. It was only this past summer that Lara had shot up the extra inches beyond her mother's five-foot-five frame. She had Sally's lean, athletic frame, only she carried a lot more muscle on it than Sally did.

"How was training?"

"Good. Hard." Lara yawned.

"Do you feel ready for the race on the weekend?" Again, Sally felt sad that she would have to miss it.

"I think so." Lara stooped to give Armani a hug, too. Then she called good-night to her father and trudged upstairs to her room.

Sally was left to face Neil on her own. Her ex-husband's handsome face had lost its smile as soon as his daughter went inside. Now he regarded Sally with an intensity that made her want to hide.

She saw him notice the pink mark on her hand, but again, he said nothing about Friday night.

"Out late were you?"

Neil specialized in doing this. Offering up tidbits of her life that he ought to have no idea about. It was one of his techniques for keeping her off balance.

For making it appear that he was in control, that he held the upper hand.

In this case, Sally could only speculate that he had felt the hood of her car and found it warm.

"I always work late on Wednesday nights." She spoke in the cool tone that she had perfected on Neil. She knew it grated on him, that he far preferred to see her visibly rattled.

Neil stepped closer and Armani whined. Soon, Sally hoped, the pup would learn to growl. She patted Armani reassuringly and held his leash a little tighter. "It's late, Neil. What time do you want Lara ready on Friday?"

He usually picked her up on his way home from work, around five-thirty. But Neil ignored her question as he moved close enough that she could see the black centers of his eyes, dilated in the weak light of her outdoor lamp.

"Since when did you start drinking when you're at work, Sal?"

He'd noticed the slight flush that even one glass of wine would bring to her cheeks. Sally did her best to maintain a stoic facade, but the truth was her ex-husband often gave her the impression of being able to read her mind.

"Out with your new boyfriend, were you? Don't you think it's time you told me his name?"

She shivered at his all too accurate conjecturing.

Colin wasn't her boyfriend. But the way she felt about him was far from just friendly. She averted her eyes so Neil wouldn't read anything else from them.

"I'll have Lara ready at five-thirty on Friday."

Neil's gray eyes narrowed. "No point in keeping secrets. You know I'll find out soon enough."

She closed the door on his parting words, wishing they hadn't sounded like some sort of threat. After turning the dead bolt, she reset the alarm, then waited for her pulse to slow to normal.

She was safe. Lara was home. All was right with the world.

As Sally peeked from behind the curtain, watching to make sure Neil really did drive away, she wished the feeling of security could last forever. But she knew that as long as Neil was part of her life, it never would.

SALLY DIDN'T HAVE TIME to read the paper the next morning, so it wasn't until she reached her office that she heard the news. As she breezed by the reception desk, Evelyn handed her a copy of the *Herald,* open to the City section.

"Take a look at the headline," Evelyn said. "But make sure you've had your coffee, first."

"Thanks. I think." Sally nodded at the young woman she'd hired after meeting her and her children at the Emergency Shelter three years ago. Stopping off in the coffee room, she filled a mug from a fresh-smelling pot, took a sip, then glanced down at the page.

The headline, in bold, capital letters, was impossible to miss. EX-HUSBAND DUMPS TRASH ON LAWN. Below the headline was a picture of a small bungalow with mounds of household trash—some of it bagged, most of it not—piled next to the front door.

Oh, no. She recognized that house. Without reading a word of the article, Sally could guess what had happened.

Maintenance Enforcement had taken action and Rick Moore wasn't pleased.

CHAPTER SIX

SALLY WAS AT HER DESK, her coffee mug was empty, and she was still staring at the *Herald's* headline when her phone rang.

"Did you see what he did?" Pamela Moore sounded frantic. "He's an animal! A filthy animal! Why would he do something like this?"

"He's trying to intimidate you, Pam." Divorce certainly brought out the worst in many people. Sally saw examples like this all too often.

As Pam ranted some more, Sally skimmed the article. *Neighbors reported seeing a man who matches the description of the resident's ex-husband arrive at midnight with a truck full of garbage. He backed up to the front door, then shoveled the trash onto the lawn...*

"Pam? Were you awake when Rick did this?"

"No, but the noise sure woke me—and our neighbors I might add—in a hurry."

"What time was it?"

"Just after midnight."

Sally jotted that down. "Did you talk to him?"

"Yelled would be more accurate. But he started it. As soon as I opened the front door he went after me."

"Physically?"

"Not this time. He was too busy shoveling garbage, I guess. Plus, at least two of my neighbors were watching by that point."

"You say Rick was yelling. Do you recall what he said?"

"That I was trash and I was going to be sorry I'd ever messed with him."

Sally copied that, word for word. "Anything else? Did he make any threats?"

"I think he said something about kicking my face in the next time I went crying to Maintenance Enforcement."

"Okay." Sally noted that, too, then set down her pen. "The last restraining order we took out on him is expired, but after this stunt, we should have no trouble getting another. I'll prepare an affidavit today. I'm glad he woke up the neighbors. Witnesses are always helpful. Do you know the neighbors' names?"

As Pam recited them, Sally made careful note.

"What about the police? Did you call them last night?"

"Sally, it all hapened so *fast*. Then, after he left,

what was the point? I figured I could handle it in the morning, but now I'm already late for work and—"

Poor Pam sounded so flustered. "I'll contact the police for you and arrange to have the trash removed. Then you can drop by the station to give your statement at your convenience." Sally paused. "How are the children?"

"They don't understand what really happened. I made up a story about a garbage truck having an accident. But when I drop them off at day-care some of the older kids are sure to tell them it was their daddy. What are they going to think about that?"

"I don't know," Sally answered honestly. More than anything, she hated that innocent children were in the middle of this. She just hated it.

"I'll call you during my lunch break, okay? I hope he goes to jail for this, I really do."

Pam hung up, leaving Sally shaking her head. For every positive action Pam took in her attempt to regain control of her life and do the best for her children, Rick took an equal and opposite negative action.

When the couple had lived together, he'd vented his frustration by punching Pam. Now he slashed tires, reneged on child-support payments…and dumped trash in his children's front yard.

What could be done with a man like this? Sally picked up the phone. She needed to talk to the police and find out what charges could be laid. Then she'd take care of having the garbage removed so Pam wouldn't have to face it all again at the end of her workday.

As she checked her records for the number of an officer she knew was sympathetic to cases like this, Sally couldn't help but think the world would be a better place if people had to answer a skill-testing question before they became parents. A dash of human kindness also wouldn't hurt.

MOST OF THURSDAY was spent sorting out the situation with Pam. Lara had a spare in the afternoon, so Sally picked her up from school early. While Lara babysat Samuel and Tabby, Sally accompanied Pam to the police station where the young mother filed a complaint, then to the Court of Queen's Bench, where they applied for the restraining order on an ex parte basis.

Given his history of violence and the threats he'd uttered in the presence of witnesses, Sally didn't think it would be wise to have Rick in the courtroom. Fortunately the judge agreed with her.

One hour later, she and her client left the court-house with documents in place.

"This is only going to make him madder than ever," Pam predicted.

Sally knew Pam had reason to feel nervous. While the restraining order prohibited Rick from coming within six blocks of Pam, in the past he had found other ways of hurting his wife. Even if he defied the order, the most likely consequence to him would be just one night in custody. Remedies under the law were so restrictive in these situations.

"I share your frustration, Pam. But we had to file the restraining order, even though it will make him angry. We can't let Rick get away with these stupid stunts of his."

"Well, I think I should have hauled that garbage to his mother's front door. That would have taught him a thing or two."

"Do you really think so?" Sally pressed the unlock button on her key chain. Once she and Pam were both seated, with belts in place, she drove back to Pam's home.

"Oh, probably not." Pam fidgeted in her seat, then let out an impatient sigh. "The truth is, he'll never change, no matter what I do. I just wish…"

Sally waited, then prodded. "What, Pam?"

"I wish he could have kept his temper under control. That we could be together as a family. You'd never guess it now, but he used to be so sweet. When I married him, I never thought I'd end up a single mom, having to raise and provide for my children on my own. My life wasn't supposed to be like this."

Mine either. Sally didn't usually think of her own

situation when she was talking to her clients, her professional sense of detachment was too well ingrained. But the emotion, the disappointment and hurt, behind Pam's words got to her.

She'd wanted so much more for Lara than to be ping-ponged between two hostile parents. At least Neil, unlike Rick, was an involved father who cared about his daughter.

But even that small blessing caused Sally worry. She was always on the lookout for signs of problems in her daughter and Neil's relationship. She'd even hired an investigator once, a few years ago, to make sure there was no hint of abuse in the way Neil treated Lara when she wasn't around.

And, thank God, there hadn't been.

She parked the car in front of Pam's bungalow, then turned to her client. "Your life will be good again, Pam. I really believe that. Let's take these problems with Rick one day at a time. Hopefully he'll come to his senses once he realizes that he could be facing a jail term if he doesn't shape up."

Sally walked Pam to the door. They found Lara and the kids playing a board game on the floor of the sparsely furnished living room. Sally was relieved to see that all three seemed in good spirits.

"I'm Lara's partner," Tabby announced proudly. "We're winning, right, Lara?"

Lara winked at Samuel, who actually had one

more man at home base than the girls. "You're really good at Trouble," she told Tabby.

"Oh, she's good at trouble, all right." Pam laughed, then planted a kiss on her daughter's pudgy cheek.

Sally was glad to see the other woman's mood lift the minute she was around her children again. "We should be going, Lara. I know you have homework."

"We'll play again, soon," Lara promised the children as she got up from the floor in one fluid motion.

Her daughter was wearing hip-hugging black pants with a wide belt and two layered tank tops. She looked sleek, toned and healthy, and Sally felt a familiar buzz of pride. Lara liked children and was good with them. This wasn't the first time she'd babysat these two.

"Thanks so much, Lara." Pam opened her purse and pulled out ten dollars.

"No, thank you, Ms. Moore." Lara politely declined the money. "I like playing with Tabby and Samuel. You don't have to pay me."

Sally smiled at her daughter. God, she was such a good kid. Why had she been mentally griping about her life in the car earlier? She was so, so lucky.

"We'll be in touch, Pam." Sally held the front door for Lara. "Let me know if you run into any problems."

"I will." Pam had scooped Tabby into her arms. She held the little girl balanced on one hip and waved as Sally and Lara drove off.

"Thank you so much for helping out," Sally said to her daughter as she navigated toward the highway home.

"No problem." Lara watched as her mother merged into the right lane of a busy freeway. "I should be the one driving, you know. I am sixteen."

Sally kept the smile on her face with effort. Why did Lara have to raise this topic when she was feeling so good right now? On second thought, Sally realized that was probably exactly why she'd brought up her driving now. Because she'd just done a favor for her mom. Good negotiating tactics, she silently congratulated her daughter.

"We've discussed this before, Lara. Once your ski season is over, I'll register you in driver's education courses. When you've completed both in-class and on-road training, I'll let you drive my car."

Lara was silent for a moment. Then she said, "Dad already lets me drive his."

"He does?" Sally shot her daughter a quick, alarmed glance, then tightened her hold on the steering wheel. She'd told Neil how she wanted to handle this. And he'd agreed. He'd agreed!

But then, he'd also gone behind her back to get Lara her learner's permit about a year ago.

"What goes on with your father doesn't affect the deal you and I made, Lara. You won't drive *my* car until you've finished the driver's-ed program."

Silently she cursed her ex-husband, not surprised, at all, that he'd subverted the plan that she'd proposed. Neil was constantly overriding her decisions and seemed to derive great pleasure from doing so. She was just thankful that he agreed with her on the big things—Lara's school, her ski program and her weekend curfew of midnight.

"Can I sign up for driving classes in a couple of weeks then? This is the last week of skiing," Lara pointed out. "We're having our end-of-the-year party Saturday night, after the race."

"Fair enough, Lara." Sally was on Highway 8 now, cruising the last kilometers toward home. She loved this section of the drive, when the city was in the rearview mirror and they had the view of the Rockies in front of them.

They'd have salad and a frozen pizza for dinner, she decided. The *Gilmore Girls* were on TV tonight and this was the one day of the week when Sally made an exception and allowed the set to be on while they were eating.

"On Monday we'll go down to the Alberta Motor Association and enroll you," Sally continued. "How does that sound?"

"Awesome, Mom. Thanks."

"You're welcome, hon." She eased the vehicle into the garage, then turned off the ignition. Lara already had the car door open.

"What's the hurry?" Sally reached for her briefcase in the back seat.

Lara paused at the doorway. "I've got to phone all my friends and tell them. They'll be so excited."

Sally shut the car door and headed toward her daughter. "Because you're taking driver's ed?"

"No, silly. Because of the car!"

Oh-oh. "Lara? What are you talking about?"

"Didn't Dad tell you? He promised when I qualify for my license, he'll buy me a BMW convertible. Isn't that cool?"

WHEN NEIL CAME to pick up Lara on Friday after school, Sally still hadn't decided how to handle the issue of the car, so she didn't raise the subject with him.

"Good luck with the race, hon." She gave Lara a tight hug. Neil had hauled off her duffel bag and was tossing it into the back seat.

With a final wave for her mom, Lara settled into the front seat of Neil's dark green Jag. The car, Sally had to admit, was a beauty. It went perfectly with the image her ex-husband presented to the world. To everyone, it seemed, but her.

He shoved his sunglasses up on his head and

leaned over the car roof to talk to her. "Coming to the race on Saturday?"

She was startled by the invitation and the charming grin that accompanied it. Neil was the one who had pointed out, several years ago, that Lara seemed to perform better when they didn't both attend the same race.

What was he up to?

"Daddy, Mom has to work this weekend." Lara leaned out the open passenger window, speaking before Sally had a chance to. "Isn't that right, Mom?"

With her daughter's eyes pleading at her, Sally was quick to nod in agreement. "Promise you'll phone me as soon as the race is over."

"We will." Lara's face brightened now that the potential crisis was over. She turned to her father, who had climbed back into the driver's seat. "Can we go to Peter's Drive-In for dinner, Daddy?"

"Whatever you want, sport."

Sally heard the car roar to life, and then they were off.

SALLY HADN'T actually picked up a knife in her kitchen since the fiasco with Neil last weekend. As she stood in front of the open fridge trying to decide what to throw together for her solitary meal, she heard a knock at the back door.

Armani started to bark, so she put him in the laundry room, then rushed back to the kitchen. Had Lara forgotten something?

But Colin Foster stood at the door. And he had a large pizza box in his hands.

"I realize I'm taking a gamble here, but I wondered...?"

She hesitated, her orderly mind already analyzing. Why was he here? Was this a smart idea? Might it not lead to something neither of them really wanted?

But if she said no, if she turned him away, she'd only sit here and stew about being alone and missing Lara's big race tomorrow.

"I think I could round up some beer to go with that." She held the door open wide.

"Great." Colin set the box down on the kitchen island, while she went to the fridge. She opened two bottles and handed him one.

"Good week?" she asked, tapping her bottle against his before taking a swallow.

"Busy. But that's the way I like it." He opened the pizza box and offered her the first slice.

They ended up in the family room, settled in the two love seats on either side of the river-rock fireplace. Over pizza they argued about who was the more valuable hockey player on the Flames team—right winger, Iginla, or Kiprusoff, the goalie.

Then Sally brewed them fresh espressos with the

built-in coffee machine and they debated the pros and cons of the two main candidates in the upcoming federal election.

Eventually their conversation shifted to work. Colin told her about an interesting trial he'd concluded that week, then she filled him in on the garbage story.

"I saw the headline in the paper this week," Colin said. "That was your client? Sounds like a terrible situation."

"Yes. Rick has a history of violence—so this latest stunt is nothing new. We filed a restraining order, but you know how effective those are. I can't help worrying about Pam and wishing I could do more to protect her and her children."

She told him about having babysat Pam when they were growing up in Medicine Hat. Then running into her, years later, at the Women's Emergency Shelter.

Colin shook his head. "What a small world. Is there any hope for the husband? Has he taken anger-management courses?"

"Yeah…but the message isn't sinking in. He doesn't deserve his two beautiful kids, that's for sure."

"Has he ever harmed them?"

"I don't think so. Not yet anyway." She sighed and carried the empty espresso cups to the kitchen.

That was the trouble with guys like Rick Moore. You never knew exactly what they were capable of until it was too late.

"He hasn't been bothering *you*, has he?" Colin asked.

Sally settled back on her love seat. "What do you mean?"

"Rick. Has he ever threatened you, personally?"

"No. Why would you think that he had?"

"Oh, I just wondered…" Colin picked up his beer and cradled it with both hands. "I mean it occurred to me that Rick might have been the one who pushed you around last Friday."

Warning bells sounded in Sally's head. "I fell, Colin. No one pushed me."

"You fell? Or you had a seizure?"

"It wasn't a seizure."

"You're sure?"

She was touched by his genuine concern. "I'm fine, Colin. Perfectly fit as of my last physical two months ago. I lost my balance when I burned my hand. That's all."

He lifted his gaze from the bottle to her eyes and she could tell he didn't believe her.

"I'd like to help, Sally. Why won't you tell me the truth?"

CHAPTER SEVEN

COLIN COULD SEE that Sally wasn't going to say another word on the subject, so he let it drop when she didn't answer his question. Still, he was frustrated. Why the big secret? Was she protecting someone?

Or did she just not want to tell *him?*

His relationship with Sally had always been emotionally precarious. Even back in the days when he and Beth saw her and Neil on a regular basis, she never seemed relaxed around him. To be honest, he'd always felt on edge around her, too.

Somehow the layers of reserve between them had been breached when he'd come to her aid on Friday. And he was glad.

"Talking to you about Beth these past couple of days…" How to put this? "It's really helped."

Sally's expression was soft with understanding. "Me, too."

"I feel like I was living in a fog—and now it's lifted. Don't get me wrong—I still miss Beth. But it's different now."

He couldn't say the rest. That being around Sally had made him feel alive again. For instance, a couple of weeks ago, he wouldn't even have noticed the view from Sally's window. Now he could appreciate the beauty of the river valley with renewed vigor.

He stood, intending to cross to the window for a better look. But a group of photographs on a shelf next to the fireplace distracted him.

He was aware of Sally watching as he picked up the most prominently displayed one. "How old is Lara here?"

"Twelve. She'd just won a race—I can't remember which one. There have been so many."

He carried the photograph to the light by the window. Lara stood on a ski hill, holding a medal of some sort in her hand. Other than her blond hair and compact, athletic build, she didn't look much like her mother. Or her father, for that matter.

"I remember Beth saying your daughter was in competitive skiing. I was on the junior ski team when I was her age. How's she doing?"

"Very well. She made the Alberta team this year."

"That's excellent. Olympic caliber, then."

"I guess so."

"You're not happy about that?"

"Don't get me wrong. Skiing is great for Lara. I'm just not sure that I want her to dedicate her entire life to the sport."

"Does Lara want to?"

"She says she does, but I worry that she's just trying to please her dad."

"I didn't think teenagers cared what their parents wanted. I have a colleague with three grown daughters. He says the teen years are the worst."

"Lara went through a bit of a difficult stage when she was thirteen and fourteen, but overall, I've been lucky. We still have fun together. Still talk. Of course, she has her moments, and sometimes it seems that her friends are more important than air."

"Any friend in particular?"

"You mean a boy? Yes, there is Chris from the ski team. I know his parents and he's a pretty good kid. But I have to admit that I'm glad their ski commitments keep them too busy to do much regular dating."

"I'll bet."

Colin put the picture back in place, then stooped to examine the others. He saw another photograph of Lara, this one more recent. Her features had changed from those of an awkward adolescent to a pretty young woman. She still didn't look much like either of her parents, but she did remind him of someone…he couldn't think who.

A third frame held a picture of Sally and Beth by the river. The best friends had their arms linked around each other's waists.

He picked that one up. "When was this taken?"

Sally came to stand beside him. He shifted marginally nearer to her as he held out the photograph.

"Let's see—I think it was shortly after Lara and I moved to this house."

Which would have been before Beth found out she was sick. Before their world had changed forever. No wonder both women wore such happy, carefree smiles.

Though on closer examination, Colin decided that Sally's was not quite as relaxed as his wife's had been. He supposed there were reasons for that. It couldn't be easy being a divorced mom as well as an ambitious lawyer. And Sally had never taken the easy route with either of the important roles in her life.

"Beth always admired your ability to be such a great mom and still handle both your work commitments and volunteer activities."

Sally stood so close the sweet scent of her perfume teased him. He could have sworn it was the same fragrance she'd worn when she was in law school.

"Did Beth really say that?"

Sally sounded gratified. Why? "Don't *you* think you're a good mom?"

She backed off a little, put her hands on her hips. "If you asked Neil, he'd say no. He wanted me to quit my job when I had Lara. He's never supported my decision to have a career as well as a child."

"Is that why the two of you divorced?"

Sally's eyes dropped. "In part, yes."

What were the other parts, Colin wondered? Sally must have talked about her failed marriage with Beth, but his wife had never passed on the details to him.

He put down the framed picture and put a hand on Sally's shoulder. He felt her tense, but she didn't move away.

"You and Neil didn't date very long before you were married."

"Neither did you and Beth. Yet you were happy."

"Yes." Had it been luck of the draw? Colin didn't think so. "Beth gave a lot to the relationship. Probably more than I did."

"In the beginning, maybe."

He knew she was referring to Beth's last months, when he'd been absolutely devoted to making the most of the small amount of time his wife had left.

But he didn't want to hash over those painful months now. Sally was standing close enough for him to kiss. And all of a sudden, that was exactly what he longed to do.

"Sally, do you ever think—"

"No."

"You didn't let me finish." Her eyes were huge

and bright and filled with awareness. She knew exactly what he'd wanted to ask her.

"The day after we made love you told me it was a mistake," he said softly, refusing to let the subject drop.

"And it was."

"Maybe then," he conceded. "But what about now?"

He wanted to kiss her so badly. He'd always found her lovely, and for years he'd fought his visceral reaction to her mere presence. But now that he felt an emotional connection building between them, the urge to pull her into his arms was even more powerful.

"You're the most fascinating woman." He touched the side of her cheek and was amazed at the perfect softness. The woman was over forty. She didn't look it and she didn't feel it.

"Colin..."

She lowered her head so he couldn't see her eyes anymore, but when he slid an arm around her waist and pulled her forward, she didn't resist. "Sally?"

If she glanced up at him, even for a second, he was going to kiss her. His heart pounded in anticipation as he reached out to raise her chin.

But she turned her face to the side.

"Sally, am I reading you wrong? I thought you wanted—"

She laughed unevenly. "Oh, I do want, Colin. I want very much."

Good. He was unbelievably relieved to hear her say that. "So do I. But I can wait, Sally. Is that what you think we should do?"

She nodded and he pulled her closer, so her head rested on his chest. She was trembling.

She wanted to wait, but he guessed it wouldn't take much persuasion for her to change her mind. How would she feel after, though? And what about him? Was he really ready for this?

Colin realized he couldn't be sure of the answer to either question. At least not yet.

ALONE IN HIS BEDROOM at home, Colin stepped out of his jeans, pulled off his T-shirt and tossed both into the hamper. What was Sally doing right now? Maybe the same thing he was—undressing for bed.

He blinked away the erotic image, then sat at the foot of his bed. As he tugged off his socks, he noticed Beth's nightstand reflected in the mirror. He paused, suddenly riveted by the reminder of the woman he'd married, when his thoughts had been so fully occupied by another.

He felt a flash of guilt, then told himself he was being ridiculous. Beth was gone. Nothing he said or did now would change that.

Though his wife was dead, her presence was still

vivid in this room. Particularly on her nightstand which he hadn't touched since her death.

Pressing his hands to his thighs, Colin stood slowly. He went around to the other side of the bed, sat on the duvet and ran a finger along the small table.

No dust. The cleaners made sure of that. At the same time, he didn't think they had moved anything. He picked up one of the figurines. The angel had been given to Beth by one of her fellow teachers. Then there was a crystal that was supposed to bring good health.

Well, it hadn't worked. None of the gifts, cards, good wishes and prayers that her friends and neighbors had given Beth had worked.

Maybe they'd work for someone else.

He went down to the basement and came back with several boxes and a black garbage bag. He put the figurines into a box then he sorted through the books.

Beth had had this annoying habit of reading several at a time. Usually something nonfiction and educational, balanced by something light and happy, and finally some work of acclaimed fiction as well. She read from these books alternately, depending upon her mood.

After checking all the titles and reading a few of the write-ups on the back cover, Colin realized he wasn't interested in any of them. He put them into the box that he intended to drop off at the nursing home he drove by every day on his way to work.

With the top of the nightstand now clear, Colin opened the drawer next. He found several tubes of creams. One for hands, one for feet, another small jar for the face. Did all a woman's body parts require a different type of moisturizer?

He opened the one for the face and took a sniff.

Beth.

The scent brought her back so vividly he almost cried. He screwed the lid back on, then, after a pause, tossed all the containers into the garbage.

At the back of the drawer, he recognized a small cedar box he'd given to Beth for Christmas many years ago. He pulled it out and found it crammed with photographs. Most were of him, or him and Beth together. There were several of Sally, as well, and a whole bunch of Lara. Reading the backs, he realized Beth had collected a school picture from every year, starting with kindergarten.

Then he saw a picture of him and Sally. It had been taken awhile ago. Before the move to Elbow Valley, but after Sally's divorce, he thought. They were sitting at opposite sides of the sofa in his and Beth's old house. He was looking at Sally and she seemed to be laughing at him.

Beth had caught something in that photograph,

Colin thought. It was clear to him that his expression held admiration. Sally's was more complicated. Reserved and yet aware, too.

He flipped the picture over. In Beth's writing was scrawled, *Colin and Sally, Christmas 1999*. This notation was curiously followed by a question mark.

Colin felt as if his heart had started to beat slower. Harder. He felt a queasy sensation in his stomach. Guilt again.

Had Beth ever guessed what had happened between him and Sally so many years ago?

The shameful sensation faded. He'd loved Beth and been completely faithful to her. The feeling of desire he'd had for Sally tonight had not been something he'd indulged when he'd been married. Beth's question mark could have meant anything. Maybe she'd been unsure of the year.

Colin slid the photo back with the others, then turned out the light to go to sleep.

SALLY SPENT all of Sunday at the office. Earlier, Lara had called to let her know she'd placed first in the race. She'd been so excited and was looking forward to the end-of-year party for the ski team. It was being held in Canmore, at a vacation home owned by parents of one of her teammates.

"Dad said we'll probably be back later than usual on Sunday."

Sally noticed there was no hint of Neil asking her approval, even though their agreement specified Lara had to be home by six to have dinner with her mother.

"Okay, hon. Can't wait to see you. I love you."

"Love you, too, Mom."

Sally replayed those last words of her daughter's as she completed the paperwork for a court case she was arguing later that week. Several hours later, Sally closed her files, then locked them in the credenza. As she logged off the computer she noticed that it was six o'clock now. Lara would be home soon; she'd better go.

On the drive to Elbow Valley, Sally found herself thinking about the dreams she'd had last night. Dreams that had focused on Colin Foster and feelings that she did not want to associate with the man who had been her best friend's husband.

On Friday night, when he'd stopped by with that pizza, she hadn't wanted him to go home. While running errands and taking care of household chores on Saturday, she'd thought about him constantly. That evening, she'd stayed home watching a movie and had tried to pretend to herself that she wasn't waiting for a knock at the door or the phone to ring.

This was so wrong.

When Beth was alive, she hadn't been troubled by these sorts of feelings about Colin. If she'd felt anything, *anything* at all for him, it had been the merest flicker—gone in a flash, not even registering in her conscious mind.

So why was he on her mind all the time now? Why did her body come to life when he was present, interpreting the most casual of touches in the most intense and sexual ways?

Sally's mind gravitated to the one answer she could live with. It was because of Beth. They'd both loved her; they both missed her dreadfully now that she was gone. Her feelings for Colin were just the misguided offshoot of all that grief and loneliness.

As soon as Sally turned on to her cul-de-sac, she noticed the Jag parked in her driveway. Damn. Hadn't Lara said they'd be late? She glanced at the time display on her dash. Only six-thirty.

Since Neil's vehicle blocked her entrance to the garage, she parked on the street and ran to the front door.

When she got inside she could hear voices. She stepped over two sets of hiking boots—Lara's and Neil's—and headed for the kitchen. Neil sat at a stool by the island while Lara poured herself a tall glass of milk.

Neil raised his eyebrows as she made her entrance. "Well." He glanced at his watch. "Finally."

"Lara said you were going to be late." She barely glanced at her ex-husband before giving her daughter a big smile and a hug. "Congratulations, hon. I'm so proud of you."

Lara's face was flushed with happiness. "It was such a great weekend, Mom. First the race, then the party at Josh's cottage. They have a pool table and a hot tub and a huge stone barbecue where they cooked the most amazing ribs."

"A hot tub…? Did you remember to pack your bathing suit?"

"Dad bought me a new one in Canmore. It's totally awesome, want to see it?"

"Later, hon." Sally watched her daughter down her drink in several long swallows. "Are you hungry or did you stop for dinner on the way home?"

"I would have fed Lara a hamburger if I'd realized you weren't going to be home." Neil glanced around the spotless kitchen. "I don't suppose you have anything planned for dinner?"

"I thought you were going to be late." Sally regretted the apologetic note in her voice the moment after she spoke.

"You weren't planning to feed your kid, just because we were delayed by half an hour? I wonder how Lara manages to survive around here." Neil was up and off his stool. He opened the fridge and started pulling out supplies. Eggs, cheese, green peppers, ham.

Sally fought back the urge to scream at him, instead speaking as calmly as she was able. "I can make her something, Neil."

"Really? Could have fooled me." He rolled up the sleeves of his shirt, then pulled down a copper frying pan from the rack over the stove. "How does an omelet sound, sport? You go relax for a minute. I'll call you when it's ready."

Lara looked anxiously from her father to her mother. "Will you help me unpack, Mom? I can show you the new bathing suit."

Sally tried to appear calm and untroubled. "Go ahead, Lara. I'll stay here and help your father."

Clearly Lara didn't want to leave them alone together, but eventually she backed off. Sally listened as she walked down the hall. At the sound of her daughter's bedroom door closing, she turned on Neil.

"What the hell do you think you're doing? This is my kitchen. I don't want you cooking in here."

Neil's eyes were cool and calm as he cracked open another egg. "That's typical, Sal. Thinking of yourself and what you want, instead of your daughter and her needs. Lara had a physically draining weekend—she needs to eat. A fit mother would have had a decent meal waiting for her when she got home. But of course, you were too busy to spend your Sunday afternoon in the kitchen. Where were you, Sal? Hanging out with the new boyfriend?"

No point in arguing. She should have known better than to assume Neil would be feeding Lara. He was always trapping her this way. Making her appear like a negligent mother, while he was the dependable one, picking up the pieces when she failed.

"I can finish the omelet." She held out her hand for the grater he'd just pulled from one of the drawers. "I'd like you to leave." She paused. "Now."

Neil evaded her attempt to grasp the grater and began working on the cheese, shredding it into a pile on the counter.

Heaven help her deal with this man. "How many times do I have to remind you that this isn't your home? You're not welcome here and you never will be."

"And how many times do I need to remind you that Lara's needs come first? I'm going to feed her, Sal, so get over it."

The look in his eyes grew colder. "In fact, why don't you just get out of the kitchen and leave me alone. If I remember correctly, the last time you tried to cook something in here, you burned yourself badly. You wouldn't want that to happen again, would you?"

CHAPTER EIGHT

THE NEXT WEEKEND, Colin felt like an idiot standing on Sally's back deck with his power drill and toolkit in hand.

"I noticed that your door only closes partway when the dead bolt is engaged," he said when she let him inside. His ploy to see her was so obvious he half expected her to roll her eyes and laugh.

Instead, she opened the door wider. "I've been meaning to fix that." She let him in, then played with the door until it was aligned correctly for the dead bolt to work properly. This left the door projecting about half an inch from the frame.

"Can you really fix this?"

"Sure."

If he'd admitted to a certain skill with splitting atoms, she couldn't have looked any more impressed.

"That would be wonderful. I've been planning to phone one of those handymen you see advertised all the time—you know, the hire-a-husband fellows— but I haven't gotten around to it, yet."

It was Saturday morning and Sally wore jeans, with the cuffs rolled to mid-calf. She had on a pink polo shirt, untucked, and bare feet. In appearance she was the absolute antithesis of her usual, lawyerly self.

Colin found it hard to stop admiring her and focus on the door.

"Can I get you a drink?" she offered. "Something to eat?"

"Maybe when I'm finished." He dropped to his knees to take a better look at the project, but when Sally moved closer to peer over his shoulder, he again found it hard to concentrate.

Maybe he'd better send her to the kitchen after all. "Actually, I am kind of thirsty."

"Oh. Good." She stood and backed away a little. "What can I get you? Beer? Iced tea? A cola?"

What would she say if he told her what he really wanted? But no. He couldn't do that.

"Water would be fine."

"Okay. Sure. Just a second."

He listened to her move around in the kitchen, opening a cupboard, then the fridge. He heard the crush of ice cubes as she pressed the button on the dispenser.

After delivering the water, Sally left him to it and the job didn't take long. When he was done, Sally insisted on replacing the water with a beer, served cold in a frosty glass. She tossed taco chips onto a plate with a small bowl of salsa in the center.

"Want to sit out on the deck for a few minutes?"

Yes, he did. Sinking into one of four sling-back chairs around a cast-aluminum table, Colin felt a sense of well-being bordering on joy. The whole world seemed tinged with sunshine from this vantage point.

"Thanks, again, Colin. The door fits perfectly now." Sally sat in the chair next to his, placing the dish of chips and dip within easy reach of both of them.

He wondered if she had any idea how much happier he was to be here with her than alone in the house that felt so empty now. He'd have cleaned her chimney for this chance.

"No problem."

Her smile was warm. "With Armani needing out every half hour, it seems I was forever fiddling with that lock."

On cue, her dog stuck his nose out from under her chair. Sally scratched her fingers down his neck and under his collar.

"I'm surprised you bother. I don't usually keep my back door locked during the day. Sometimes I even forget to lock it at night."

Sally was still looking down at the dog. "I guess it's different when you're a woman living on her own."

Was that why Sally had a state-of-the-art security system in her home? Because she was a woman? He suspected there was more to her concern than that. Her refusal to meet his eyes confirmed it.

If only she would tell him what had happened that Friday night. But he knew better than to mention the topic again. He didn't want to cloud this afternoon with an argument. So he cast his mind for a subject they could discuss with equanimity.

"How's your client doing? The one who had garbage dumped all over her front yard?"

Sally wrinkled her nose. "What a disgusting maneuver that was. Pam was so disappointed when all the police did was charge Rick with littering. Littering! Can you believe it?"

She picked up a chip, dipped a corner into the salsa, then stared at it as if she had no idea of what to do next. "When it comes to spousal abuse, Colin, our legal system falls terribly short."

"Maybe it's human nature that we really ought to be disappointed in. I've always found it ironic that in situations of violent crime, the people closest to the victim are usually the ones to blame."

"Lashing out at the ones we love. Yes, it is a terrible human failing. I wish there was more society could do to help."

Colin found himself remembering something Beth had told him once. That Sally had decided to specialize in family law because of her own personal demons. Now he wondered just what those demons had been.

Sally's own family? Oddly, he knew little about them. There'd been no pictures of grandparents in the family room, he remembered. Was that significant?

To ask Sally now, in the middle of this conversation about abuse, would be too obvious.

Colin took a drink of his beer. "When I was growing up, I remember dreading the family dinners at my Uncle Ray's. He used to treat his wife like dirt, ordering her around and insulting her. It wasn't until I was older that I realized why my aunt always wore long sleeves and turtlenecks even in the summer."

"Did anyone in your family help her?"

"I think my parents tried. But there was so little understanding of the cycle of abuse back then. I remember overhearing my father asking my mother, *well, why doesn't she leave him, then?* I'm sure he was talking about my Uncle Ray and his wife. He sounded so frustrated and I remember thinking it was strange that he seemed more angry at my aunt than my uncle."

Sally brushed her hair back from her forehead. "That's the kind of thinking women in that situation run into far too often."

Colin leaned forward, hoping that she was about to open up about her own past.

"I had a client once—" she began, and he sagged back into his chair with disappointment. Before she could carry on with her story, the door he'd recently fixed flew open.

"Mom! Want to see my new bathing suit?"

Lara dashed out to the porch. Wow, that smile. Colin was amazed he'd never noticed it before. But then, Lara was growing up so fast. He guessed she'd grown three inches since the funeral. She'd also filled out—something the bathing suit did little to conceal.

Lara lurched to a stop when she noticed him, her excitement cooling to a mild embarrassment.

"I didn't know we had company."

"Hi, Lara." Not wanting to focus on her body in that bathing suit, he lowered his eyes. She was wearing flip-flops on her feet, and he saw that Sally hadn't been kidding. Her feet really were very long and narrow. "Sorry if I startled you. I just finished fixing the lock on the door for your mom."

Though they saw each other rarely, Lara knew him, of course. She nodded hello shyly, then backed toward the house.

Colin turned to Sally, expecting her to say something to her daughter to smooth over the awkward silence. But Sally just sat there, her lips slightly parted, her body frozen, until Lara was gone.

"Is something wrong?" he asked.

"I can't believe Neil let her buy that bathing suit." A red flush settled over Sally's light complexion. "Did you notice how revealing it was?"

He cleared his throat, suddenly fixated by the sight of his hands on the patio table. "Well, it was a little, um, rather…"

The words *itsy-bitsy, teensy-weensy* came to mind, but he kept them to himself.

"I could shoot that man, sometimes," Sally muttered.

At that point, Colin decided it was really best that he leave.

COLIN HAD THOUGHT there was something familiar about Lara's smile and now he knew what it was. After driving home from Sally's he went straight to his study. On the bottom book shelf he found the albums his mother had given him when she'd sold the family home after the divorce.

The more recent pictures, where his parents looked like old people, not the mom and dad he remembered from his youth, were no help. He flipped back to the earlier days and stopped cold when he came to the close-up of his parents taken on their wedding day.

That smile. His mother's smile: wide mouth, generous lips, a slight overbite. That was what he'd recognized in Lara.

After staring at the picture for several minutes, Colin put the album away. This was probably a co-incidence he knew…but his mind raced the way it always did when he was faced with a new piece of relevant evidence.

Like her feet. He'd only had a quick glimpse of them on the porch that afternoon but it was enough to see that they were amazingly like his.

Oh Lord. Could all this be coincidence?

If so, there was another. Lara's prowess at skiing. As far as he knew, neither Neil nor Sally were par-ticularly athletic. But he'd always excelled at sports. Baseball in the summers as a kid. And skiing in the winter.

He straightened and paced to the window and back.

Sally had been pregnant with Lara when she and Neil were married. That hadn't been any secret, es-pecially since the baby had been born only four or five months later.

Was it possible she'd been conceived on that night they were together?

Hell. His mind felt like it was ablaze. He couldn't stand still. This was crazy, wasn't it? He couldn't possibly be Lara's father.

The correct answer had to be no. For one thing, Sally would have told him.

Colin decided that the first step was to figure out

the timeline. If it turned out that he couldn't physically have been Lara's father, then he would just have to accept that the similarities between him and Sally's daughter really were plain coincidence.

In order to complete the timeline, though, he needed Lara's birth date. Beth would have known, but he didn't have a clue. He wasn't even sure of the season, let alone the month.

He cringed at the idea of asking Sally. There had to be a better way.

SUNDAY MORNING Colin noticed that the lawn in the backyard was turning green. Didn't Beth usually get the lawn people out to fertilize at this time of year? He went to the kitchen drawer where she had stuffed her little notes and business cards and, despite the clutter, soon found the number he was looking for.

He also found something else. A small, bound book with a copy of Monet's *Water Lilies* on the cover. The book was titled *Birthday Calendar.*

He'd never heard of such a thing, but his heart was pounding with anticipation as he opened the cover. Sure enough, the book was filled with Beth's neat handwriting. She had birth dates here for all their friends and family...including many people he didn't even know. Maybe her colleagues from work?

Flipping through to September, he finally found the name he was looking for. Lara Stowe Anderson had been born on September 3. Interestingly, her mother's birth date was just one day earlier, on the second.

Colin snapped the book shut and returned it to the drawer. He'd call the lawn guys later. Right now he had some research that couldn't wait.

In his study, Colin typed four carefully selected words into the search engine on his computer. Within seconds a variety of sites offering to calculate his pregnancy due date popped up on the screen. His fingers were trembling a little as he moved the mouse to one of them and double-clicked.

The computer asked him to type in the first day of his last period. Hell, he had no idea about that. All he knew was Lara's birth date. He scrolled up the page and finally found the information he needed.

Apparently, you could calculate the date your baby would be born by adding 280 days to the first day of your last menstrual period. The 280 days represented the usual 266-day gestation period, plus fourteen days.

Okay. So all he needed was to count back 266 days from September 3, right? And that would be the probable date of conception.

Colin moved back to the search box and found a site with a perpetual calendar. Counting back the days in that final year of university, he came to the probable date that Lara was conceived: December 12.

He closed down the computer and went to the window. The greening grass held no interest for him now—none at all.

Could he really be the father of a child? A sixteen-year-old daughter he hardly knew?

Though he couldn't remember the exact date he'd slept with Sally, the second week of December was in the right ballpark.

Jeez, wouldn't that be something?

His stomach clenched around the possibility the way his hand had closed tight around a baseball years ago as a boy. Full of hope and anxiety.

The realization that a part of him actually wanted this to be true, wanted him to be Lara's father, was shocking. But it was true. Imagining that he might have played a part in bringing that beautiful, healthy girl into this world—that she might be linked to him, even only biologically—was a joyful thought.

It was also a thought without any real grounding in reality.

Colin moved from the window to his favorite chair with a sigh. Just because it was physically possible for him to be Lara's father didn't mean he was.

Besides, if he *had* fathered Sally's child, surely this many years wouldn't have passed without either him or Sally—worse yet, Neil—figuring it out.

Let it drop, he counseled himself. Weren't all of their lives complicated enough already?

CHAPTER NINE

BETH HAD NEVER BEEN particularly tidy, and her car was a poignant example of this. Clearing out the clutter in the front seat of the Miata the next Saturday morning, was like a walk down memory lane. Colin had been gearing up for the task since sorting out the nightstand. He could do this, he told himself, armed with a garbage bag and a couple of damp rags. He really could.

But it was harder than he'd anticipated. A Tim Hortons bag with one stale timbit reminded him of countless times they'd pulled in to the store in West-hills after their usual Saturday-afternoon shopping excursions for coffee and a treat.

Then he found a piece of paper with the instructions to a friend's house where they'd gone to dinner almost a year ago. Since he'd been working late, Beth had met him there.

Stuffed under the passenger seat was a package of new panty hose, an unused candle, a small emergency medical kit, a well-thumbed paperback.

Beth had always striven to be prepared for any situation.

Colin transferred the medical kit to the trunk of his own car, but both the book and the candle were too battered to save. As he threw out the detritus of his dead wife's traveling life, he paused over the panty hose. Could Sally make use of these?

He read the size information on the corner of the package and considered the recommended height and weight. Though Beth had been shorter and a little rounder than her friend, the hose might just fit.

He set the package to the side, then used a rag to wipe down the dashboard and interior windows. Other than a little dust, there wasn't much to clean. Overall, the Miata was in excellent condition. It ought to sell quickly, he hoped. He was supposed to bring it in to the Mazda dealership around noon.

Which raised the problem of how he would get home.

He could take a taxi. Or, he could bum a ride from a friend. It made sense, he convinced himself, to ask someone from the same neighborhood. Suddenly smiling, he tossed the package of panty hose into the air then went inside to find the phone.

SALLY WAS NOT LOOKING forward to her Saturday chores. First on the list was laundry, followed by grocery shopping, then errands. Armani needed another bag of dog food and that required a special trip to a store on the other side of town.

Besides all that, she had to wash her car. A heavy spring snowstorm earlier in the week had melted in one day, filling the streets with muck. Now she could hardly see a trace of the original blue paint on her Outback Wagon. Friday night, on her way out the door with her father, Lara had traced "wash me" on the rear window.

Sally's lethargy deepened as she thought of her daughter's absence.

On the weekends when she had Lara, her chores didn't seem so bad. She could usually coerce her daughter into coming to the shops with her by promising to stop at the music store, then Starbucks for a Frappacinno.

But it was Neil's weekend again, it always seemed to be Neil's weekend, even though they alternated fairly. So she would have to go through the day alone and the night, too. Maybe she could make some headway with the novel she was supposed to have read for her next book-club meeting.

The prospect of curling up with a novel and a glass of wine did not seem as appealing as usual, though.

What was the matter with her? Sally dumped a load of whites into the washer, then snagged the shopping list from the magnetized pad on the side of the fridge. Lately, she'd felt so unsettled. She hadn't even found the strength to take Neil on about the bathing suit or the convertible, yet. She couldn't keep putting off that conversation. Hopefully she'd get a moment alone with him on Sunday night.

Sally was just reaching for her purse when the phone rang. She glanced over her shoulder at the call display. *Colin Foster.*

She hadn't seen him since he'd fixed her door last weekend. She'd assumed he'd come to the same conclusion that she had.

It was too soon. In fact, the timing might never be right. She didn't want to fall in love with her best friend's husband. He had to be feeling exactly the same qualms.

The phone rang a second time. A third. If he'd dialed her number just one minute later, she would have left for her errands already. She could still leave now. He'd have no way of knowing that she'd run out on his call.

But in the middle of the fourth ring, she couldn't stop herself. She picked up the receiver. "Hello?"

Darn, she sounded breathless, as if she'd dashed to catch the call, when in actual fact she'd been standing only a few feet away.

"Sally? I have a favor to ask of you."

Her heart tripped like a teenager's. "Oh?"

He explained the situation. Something about wanting to sell Beth's Miata and needing a ride home from the Mazda dealership on Macleod Trail. Nothing to do with her or what had almost happened between them the other night, just a very ordinary sort of favor. A relief and a disappointment, packaged as one.

"I need to go in that direction for dog food, anyway, Colin. I'll be glad to help."

EVERY TIME SHE SAW HIM, the sexual awareness was stronger than the time before. Like a bee-sting allergy, in a way, Sally thought, as she pushed her sunglasses up on her head.

They'd dropped the Miata off at the dealership about half an hour ago, neither of them giving word to what she knew they'd both been thinking. *Beth had loved that car so much….*

But it was gone now. The manager already had a buyer lined up when they'd arrived. Colin had seemed surprised and for a minute Sally had wondered if he was going to change his mind and keep the car. But all he'd done was open the trunk and remove a set of jumper cables and a travel blanket.

Sally was the one who'd noticed the small package wrapped in paper covered with balloons. "Is this a gift for someone?"

Colin took the box from her, looking confused.

"What the heck—?" He found a tag, then flipped it over to read the inscription. "Hell. Put this in your car, would you, please? I need to finish up here."

Then he'd gone into the office to sign the papers. Sally had done as he'd asked, avoiding the temptation to read the tag herself. Ten minutes later, Colin slipped into the passenger seat of her car.

"Okay," he'd said. "We're done."

Next, they'd stopped to pick up the dog food, then Colin had insisted on washing her car for her at one of the do-it-yourself places. She'd sat in the driver's seat of the Subaru, watching him working diligently and trying not to notice the muscles on his arms, the nice fit of his jeans, the way his hair curled a little around his ears.

She didn't often allow herself to dwell on regrets, but she had a few then. Washing the car was a relatively simple job, but it was so nice to sit back and let someone else handle the responsibility for a change. She could get used to having a man around the house again, she thought. If he was the right man.

When he'd rinsed off the last of the soap bubbles, Colin returned the wand to its holder, then settled back into the passenger seat of her wagon.

"Looks a lot better," he said.

And she thought, *yeah, you do*. How had she managed to pass so many years seeing him casually, as Beth's husband, yet never really seeing Colin, the man? Her awareness of his presence now could not have been more acute. She noticed every movement, every breath, every look.

He must be doing the same with her. She could feel him watching her now. She tried to concentrate on the turn from Macleod Trail onto Glenmore. Traffic was awful with vehicles backed up to get into Chinook Mall. She was forced to stop and wait for the cars ahead of her to move.

"Busy time of day," Colin commented.

She continued to look ahead, not daring to meet his gaze. "Calgary's growing so fast."

The trite phrases did nothing to ease the tension she was feeling. Did Colin sense it, too? He was so big, his presence overpowered her small, utilitarian vehicle. His thigh was just a foot away from hers. His knees collided with the dash.

"So what was that package?" she asked, nodding toward the back seat, where she'd placed the gift he'd removed from Beth's trunk.

"Apparently it's mine."

"What?"

"She must have bought it in advance for my birthday."

"That sounds like something Beth would do." But how hard it must have been. Shopping for a gift, knowing you would be gone by the time the occasion for it to be opened came along.

Sally swallowed an urge to cry. The car in front of them inched forward, and Sally followed. When she was stopped again, she turned toward Colin. "When's your birthday?"

"This Wednesday."

"Really? That's amazing timing."

"Beth would have guessed I wouldn't be able to clean out her car right away." He shook his head. "She knew the way I procrastinate when I really don't want to do something."

Sally chuckled. "That's right. I remember her saying that the Christmas tree would come down in June if she left it up to you."

"Miserable job taking down Christmas trees."

"I couldn't agree more." The congestion in front of them eased enough for Sally to slip into the left-hand lane. Suddenly they were moving again, catching the next light green, then speeding forward onto the freeway.

As the car accelerated, so did their conversation. By the time Sally had parked in front of Colin's home, she felt comfortable again. The earlier moments of intense awareness had passed.

"Thanks for the ride, Sally." Despite his words, Colin seemed in no rush to get out of her car.

"I managed to knock two items off my to-do list as well."

"That's good." He cleared his throat. "Maybe that means you'll have a little free time tonight?"

Just like that, her nerves returned. She gripped the steering wheel tightly and kept her head forward. "And if I do?"

"I was thinking…would you like to go out to dinner?"

IT WAS SATURDAY NIGHT and she had a date. Sally stood in front of the full-length mirror in her bedroom and recalled the last time she'd gone out with a man.

It had been this past New Year's Eve, more than four months ago. The man had been another attorney, recently divorced. The evening had gone well, but Sally had turned down a follow-up invitation for dinner at his place the next weekend.

He'd seemed too eager to get her to bed, and she could guess why. Confidence frazzled by his wife's betrayal, he'd been anxious to prove his prowess as a lover. A cynical assessment, perhaps, but the problem was, after all these years in family law she knew men—and their reactions to divorce—all too well.

Sally swiveled in her black dress, checking her hose from both sides and the rear. She looked good, darn good, and suddenly she felt an effervescent shot of nerves in her stomach.

The problem with Colin was that he mattered so much. She couldn't blow this evening off as just another date. If it didn't go well, she knew she'd be devastated. On the other hand, if the date was a success, she'd be almost as upset.

She didn't want to get involved with the man who had been Beth's husband. Colin was last person she would have chosen to fall for.

But she couldn't deny that that was exactly what was happening. How else could she explain why she turned gaga when she was around him?

The doorbell rang and Armani started to bark. Sally slipped on her sling-back shoes and grabbed the matching clutch purse. She'd seen Colin in a suit a hundred times, but observing him on her doorstep in his best charcoal Hugo Boss, she definitely went weak in the knees. She hid her vulnerability by leading Armani to the laundry room.

"I won't be long," she told the dog on their way out.

"Don't count on that," Colin said.

Or did he? Sally's heart was pounding so loudly she couldn't be sure she heard him correctly.

COLIN HAD ALWAYS LOVED Sally in her little black cocktail dress. He'd seen her wear it on a number of occasions, but never before had the sight of her long, slender legs and hint of cleavage affected him so instantly, so profoundly.

She's got me tied up in knots.

The realization was no comfort as he backed his vehicle out of her driveway and headed for the restaurant he'd chosen for the night.

"Isn't this the wrong way?" Sally asked, when he turned left, rather than right, onto the highway.

"I thought we'd go to Bragg Creek." The quaint mountain town, nestled into a coniferous forest in the foothills, was a twenty-minute drive in the opposite direction from Calgary.

"Good idea."

Hard as it was to believe, Sally sounded almost as nervous as he felt. This first-date business was unbelievably hard. What he needed to do, Colin realized, was find some way to set them both at ease.

He knew just the topic.

"So how was work last week?"

"Not as busy as usual. For right or wrong, Gerald is assuming I'm going to get that judicial appointment next month so he's discouraging me from accepting new cases. In fact, I've been parceling out most of my pending files to my colleagues."

"What about the woman whose husband dumped that garbage on her lawn?"

"Pam's going to be tough. I've been handling her work pro bono. Despite the fact that we knew each other when we were younger, it was hard for me to earn her trust. I can't hand her case over to just anyone."

"What's been going on with her lately?" He noticed Sally uncross her arms and lean back into her seat, and allowed himself a small smile. The topic of work wouldn't relax every woman but it sure worked with Sally.

"Pam's life is a constant soap opera. Last week we filed a restraining order after Rick's stunt with the garbage. I was expecting another retaliatory move from him, but so far there's been nothing. Pam's on pins and needles. I'm hoping that maybe, finally, Rick has decided to grow up."

Colin took his eyes off the road for a moment. "You think it's possible?"

"In my experience it doesn't happen as often as it should, but it does happen."

A few hours later, Colin reflected that his strategy to set them both at ease by talking shop had worked too well. Dinner was over and they were back in the car headed home, and still talking about the law.

Sally had worked them all the way back to university days.

"Admit it, Colin. You were an arrogant SOB. You can't blame me for trying to knock you down a peg or two."

"You think *I* was the arrogant one? In class you were always the first with an answer." She'd spent almost every free hour at the library—this hot blonde with the great legs, who wouldn't give a guy the time of day unless he happened to know of an interesting precedent.

"That's because I studied hard. But you. You would show up to class obviously hungover. It was clear to everyone that you hadn't cracked a book all night. And yet, when the prof picked on you, you always had the audacity to argue your way into the right answer."

"That's because I have an instinct for the law."

She laughed. "An instinct for the law? I love your confidence. You had a rich father and no fear of flunking out like the rest of us."

He couldn't believe this. "You think I scraped by on favoritism?"

"No, no. You knew your stuff. It was just…surprising that you spent all your time partying and still got such great grades."

"You really didn't like me, did you?"

She considered that a moment. "Not really. No."

He slowed the car as he drew near to the turnoff. "Because I was smart?"

"Because you didn't appreciate your advantages."

Her tone, when she'd first raised the subject of their student days, had been teasing. Now he sensed a real frustration in her voice. Something more was going on here. He turned at the four-way stop and followed the road to her street. Only one light was on inside her house. Probably the laundry room for Armani. He turned off the ignition.

"There was one night when you didn't seem to mind my advantages."

Though it was too dark to see her expression, he heard her sharp intake of breath.

"Bringing up that night isn't fair, Colin."

"Why not? You're the one who gave me the boot when it was over. If anyone should be holding a grudge about that night—"

"I'm not holding a grudge. But I think this might be a good time to say good-night. Thanks for dinner, Colin." She opened the car door and made a quick escape.

Shocked, it took Colin a moment to follow her. He couldn't let the night end this way.

"Sally, I was crazy about you in law school. It made me insane the way I couldn't seem to do anything right in your eyes." He'd followed her to the front door. Now, as she struggled with the keys in the dark, he took them from her and unlocked her door.

She rushed inside, leaving him out on the stoop.

"I'm sorry," he said, feeling miserable. How had this night ended so badly? He'd had such high hopes. Now Sally was furious at him. And he didn't even understand why.

His apology seemed to have the right impact, though. Sally appeared stunned by it. She looked him deeply in the eyes, then sighed. "You have nothing to be sorry about. I was crazy about you, too."

And then she kissed him.

CHAPTER TEN

ONCE BEFORE Sally had felt like this…caught up in emotions that she simply couldn't comprehend. Colin frustrated her, astounded her, amused her, challenged her. But overriding all of that right now was the way he made her weak with longing.

Sixteen years ago he'd pulled her into his arms and over the threshold of his off-campus apartment. Now she did the same to him. Colin seemed to have no objection to being kissed without warning; in fact, he soon took the initiative himself, and Sally thrilled at the sensation of being enveloped by him.

Somehow the front door closed and Colin leaned against it for support as he all but lifted her off the ground in his efforts to hold her ever closer.

This was no gentle good-night kiss, no exploratory move to see what the next step should be. For a few insane moments, Sally felt no boundary between herself and Colin as latent need burst into hot, physical reality. She felt his breath, his lips, his tongue, as he moved from her mouth to claim the tender spot behind her ear, then her neck, then her shoulder.

She was ready for him to work his way right down her entire body.

And then she heard Armani whimpering from the laundry room. Suddenly she was Sally Stowe, LLB, QC, again. Divorced mother of Lara, contender for Justice of the Court of Queen's Bench and dog owner.

Her arms went from pulling Colin closer to offering a gentle resistance. "Armani. He needs out."

"What?"

Colin was still in the trance that she'd been under. His eyes were glazed as he pulled back to look at her questioningly. Slowly what she'd said sank in.

"Is he in the laundry room?"

Too breathless to speak, Sally nodded. Her dress had somehow ridden up her thighs and now she pulled it back down her legs.

"I'll get him." Colin ran a hand tenderly along her cheek, then turned for the hallway.

Sally flicked on the lights, then picked her purse and keys from the floor. As she set them in the closet, Armani came barreling for her, his entire body wiggling with pleasure.

"Good boy, Armani, good boy. Did you miss me?"

Armani gave her a kiss, then began to whine again.

"He needs outside," she said.

Colin followed her as she passed through the great room to the kitchen, then the back door. She let the dog out into the fenced yard and stood at the open door watching as he chose a spot to relieve himself.

A few seconds later, she felt Colin's warmth behind her. He placed a hand on her shoulder. She stayed facing the yard, afraid that Colin might expect them to pick up where they'd left off.

Not that her body wasn't still humming with desire for him. It was.

But their kiss tonight could not end in the same way their kiss sixteen years ago had.

"Don't worry, Sally. I'm not going to pressure you."

She said nothing, but she could feel some of the tension leave her body.

"Yes, I want to make love with you tonight, but I know it's too soon."

"Too soon?"

"Eventually it's going to happen, though," he said.

Just out of habit, she wanted to disagree. As if sensing her reaction, he lowered his voice.

"Or don't you want it to?"

She wanted it. She wanted him. Now and sixteen years ago and maybe all the years in between, as well. Because of Beth, she'd suppressed all of that.

It hadn't always been easy. As she and Neil had fought their way through those first years of marriage, then through the bitter stages of their divorce, she'd looked at Beth and Colin and it had been hard not to feel envious.

Fate was so capricious. Why couldn't she have realized she was attracted to Colin just one month earlier—before he'd even met Beth?

But Sally didn't allow herself to think that way often. What kind of person resented her own best friend's happiness?

So she'd ruthlessly pushed those feelings for Colin from her mind until feigning disinterest in the man had become ingrained in her system.

"Sally?" Colin's hands skimmed down the sides of her body. "Tell me what you want."

Indifference was impossible now. These past weeks she'd begun to feel the force of her attraction to Colin on all levels. Emotional, physical and intellectual. Everything pointed to the inevitability of their being together.

And yet it wouldn't be an easy step to take. Not only because of Beth, but her own situation was difficult, too. Since her divorce, all her attempts at romantic relationships had been doomed to failure.

"Colin, I feel the same way you do. But this is complicated."

"I agree." With gentle pressure to her shoulders,

he swiveled her to face him. "I'm all for going slowly. Just as long as I can continue to see you. What about tomorrow? Let's take a walk along the river, then come back to my place for lunch."

Overwhelmed by the wish to say yes, Sally had to close her eyes in order to shake her head. "I can't, Colin. I always go to the office on Sundays when Lara's with Neil."

"Didn't you say work was slow right now?"

"There are things I need to do." Not really, but she had to slow him down somehow. She dared another glance at Colin, but it was hard to keep her resolve with him standing so close, touching her shoulders.

She broke away and crossed the room to the kitchen where she poured a couple glasses of water. She kept one for herself, then put the other on the island for him.

"So when can we see each other again? Friday night?"

"I have Lara next weekend."

"Won't she have plans with friends in the evening?"

"Probably." In fact, Lara had already asked if she could go to a girlfriend's for a sleepover on Friday, then to a movie with Chris on Saturday.

"So…?" Colin waited expectantly.

"This isn't the best time for us to start dating. Maybe in a month or two." She turned her head away from the hurt expression on Colin's face. If only he would take her rejection at face value and back off for a while.

"A month or two. Am I missing something here? Are you trying to give me the brush-off?"

He moved closer and again she averted her head. "Why won't you look at me?"

"It's just that my life is complicated."

"Is this about Beth?"

"Only partly."

"Sally, I understand that you have a daughter and a career, but so do a lot of unmarried women your age. What's so complicated?"

"Well, there's Neil for one thing." Oh no. She shouldn't have said that. Colin's eyes took on a lawyerly gleam. Leaning over the island, he tried to capture and hold her attention.

"What does your ex-husband have to do with you and me?"

Now she had to explain. But would Colin understand? "Since our divorce there have been a few men I've tried dating on a regular basis."

"And—?"

"Neil always reacts badly. I can't explain why. He didn't want the divorce in the first place and sometimes he acts like he's still married to me."

"How can you put up with that?"

There it was. The question she couldn't answer,

no matter how often she tried. "I do fight him on some things, Colin. But he's a great father to Lara and I don't want to cause waves when it isn't necessary."

"I take it you would classify dating me as creating unnecessary waves?"

"It's the timing. Once Willa's replacement has been named, whether I get the appointment or not, it won't matter so much."

Colin reached over the island to clasp her hand. "You're implying that you're afraid of making Neil angry in case he does something to jeopardize your appointment?"

She let out a long breath. "Yes."

"But that's crazy. Yes, Neil's a successful lawyer, but he doesn't wield omniscient power over the legal profession."

Colin still didn't get it. She pulled her hand away and stared into the glass of water. "I'm not talking about things he would do through legitimate channels."

"Then what—?" Colin straightened to his full height as comprehension lit his face. "That Friday night. It was Neil, wasn't it? He's the one who hurt you."

"I can't talk about this anymore." Sally crossed the room to let Armani back into the house. She turned the dead bolt, which worked like a charm thanks to Colin.

"Sally. Look at me. If Neil hurt you—"

"I've already told you—it was an accident." She still didn't believe Neil had meant to go that far. "Colin, you need to leave now."

"But I'm worried about you. If Neil is violent—"

"He isn't."

"Then why won't you go out with me?"

"Like I said earlier, it's complicated."

"Sally, this is so not like you. Do you really intend to let the man you divorced thirteen years ago dictate your love life?"

"Neil doesn't dictate my love life." But even as she made the denial, she knew it was false. She didn't want to believe Neil had that sort of power over her. But he did.

"God, Sally, don't you see how insane this is?"

"Of course I do. But you don't know Neil…what he's capable of…."

Colin gripped her shoulder. "I can handle Neil."

Oh, if only it could be that simple. But Sally couldn't give in to the fantasy of having another man solve all her problems. With Neil there was no solution. Just bargaining tactics.

"I'm sorry, Colin. I realize this doesn't make sense to you. But I know what I'm doing. For some reason Neil's having trouble coming to terms with this judicial thing. He's always resented my career successes. I guess he thinks that they detract from the time I spend with Lara. But he'll come to terms with this and when he has, then I think you and I can—"

Colin waved off her rationalizations. "I don't like what I'm hearing. I don't want you to be alone with this guy. Ever. I want to be here with you when he comes around."

"Colin, I appreciate the sentiments, but it isn't your place to try and protect me. Besides, your presence would only aggravate the situation. Trust me. I know how to handle Neil."

And Colin didn't. It was as simple as that.

THE MORE SALLY TOLD HIM about Neil's behavior, the more Colin's protective instincts became engaged. He didn't want to leave her alone, but when she insisted he go home, he had no choice but to do as she asked.

Had Beth fully comprehended what a bastard Sally's ex was? He'd heard his wife complain about Neil every now and then, but he'd never paid much attention. He'd assumed that Sally and Neil had the usual post-divorce complaints and headaches.

He'd never guessed Neil was controlling and emotionally abusive. And possibly physically abusive, too.

Sally might not agree with the labels, but from his perspective they sure seemed to fit.

From the driver's seat of his vehicle, he watched

as the main room lights flicked off in her house, leaving just a warm glow from Sally's room. He pictured her stepping out of her high heels, sliding the little black number down her body.

Lord, he wanted her. But he couldn't let desire cloud his judgment. Sally needed his help, even though she wouldn't admit it. But what could he do when she was so determined to handle this on her own?

Finally her bedroom light dimmed and Colin realized there was no point in him parking in her driveway all night. She had good locks, a security system and a dog. She was as safe as could be.

He turned on the ignition and backed out to the street. He drove home reluctantly, and when he got there, his house seemed bigger and more empty than ever.

He went to the fridge for a drink. Judith's lentil-and-bean casserole, covered in foil, caught his eye. He really had to talk to that woman. Soon.

Colin snagged the beer he'd been after, then retreated to his study. Really, this was the only room he needed. Why had he and Beth purchased such a large place?

Because they'd planned on having a family. A family that had never materialized.

For the first time, Colin wished he knew why. Was it Beth's problem or his? If it had been his, if he had a low sperm count or something, then that would be the ultimate proof that he wasn't Lara's father.

Of course, there were other ways to find out the truth. He could start by asking Sally. But she wouldn't necessarily know.

Which left…DNA testing. There was a company he used regularly for work purposes. He didn't necessarily want to go to them with a private matter, though.

Colin crossed the room to his desk. The computer was ready and waiting. Once he'd connected to the Internet, he opened the search engine and typed in *"paternity testing."*

A long list of possibilities were suddenly before him.

NEIL DIDN'T EVEN get out of the car when he dropped Lara off on Sunday night. He was right on time…six o'clock. He drove away with one final wave for his daughter, and Sally realized she'd have to postpone the discussion about Lara's convertible and skimpy bathing suit, yet again.

She thought she'd get her chance on Wednesday, but Neil picked Lara up from school and left a message saying he wouldn't have her home until after nine.

Now that Sally's caseload was so slack she had no excuse to stay late at the office. Instead, she went home and baked a lasagna. She cheated a little, using jarred tomato sauce, a package of grated cheese and the type of noodles that didn't need to be precooked. But she felt it could still be billed honestly as home-made.

When the casserole had finished baking, she decided to take a chance and drop in on Colin without phoning ahead. She found him home; he answered the door mere seconds after she hit the doorbell.

"Happy Birthday, Colin. I baked you a lasagna."

It was a warm May evening and he was wearing a pair of faded navy shorts and a baggy white T-shirt. From the green stains on his toes, Sally guessed he'd just finished mowing the lawn.

She felt suddenly nervous about showing up this way. "You said you liked anything with a tomato sauce. So I thought, for your birthday…"

Finally he smiled. "Sally, you amaze me." He held out his hands for the protective wicker basket. "You'll join me, I hope?"

She relaxed with relief that she hadn't somehow made a misstep in their precarious relationship. "Wouldn't be a party if you were on your own," she agreed.

Colin opened a bottle of Chianti and they ate at the kitchen table. Sally could see the unopened gift from Beth sitting on the counter by the coffee-maker.

Between mouthfuls, Colin commented, "I take it this isn't a date. Since we're not doing that."

She considered the appropriate label. "A dinner between friends."

"I guess that'll do. For now."

Though his voice held the promise of something much more exciting, he continued to concentrate on his meal. When they were both finished, he unwrapped the gift from Beth and found a biography. "Beth knew I wanted to read this."

Below the title page was inscribed a message. "Be well, Colin. Love, Beth."

Sally made a pretense of going to the washroom to give Colin time to recover. Herself, too.

Oh, Beth. Am I doing the right thing? Should I even be here right now? She couldn't believe Beth would want Colin to be alone on his birthday. But would she approve of him and Sally becoming such good friends? Would she have approved of them becoming more than that?

Sally rinsed her hands and wondered what it would be like to live her life without worrying what other people thought. Since her marriage and almost even more since her divorce, she'd grown accustomed to factoring Neil's wishes into all but the most trivial of decisions.

Now she was worrying about what Beth would think of her relationship with Colin. At work she was constantly second-guessing her decisions, remembering Willa's warning: once you send in that application, she'd told Sally, you will be under the closest scrutiny you have ever experienced.

Of course Willa didn't know what it was like to be Neil Anderson's ex-wife.

Sally returned to the kitchen and found Colin almost finished the washing up. The coffee machine on the counter had just completed its cycle.

Sally opened the fridge for the cream and found a chocolate layer cake front and center. "Wow. Did you buy this?"

Colin shifted so she couldn't see his face. "A colleague baked that for me."

A colleague. Sally smiled. "Is she pretty?"

"She has cats. About a dozen."

A dull red stain was creeping round his neck. Well, well, well. Interesting how easy it was to make the mighty crown prosecutor blush. Sally moved the cake to the counter, then took plates from a cupboard, a knife from the drawer by the stove. She knew Beth's kitchen almost as well as she knew her own. She had the knife poised over the center of the cake, when Colin realized what she was doing.

"Don't cut that!"

"Why? Did you want me to sing 'Happy Birthday' first?"

He blushed again. "Of course not. It's just that we can't eat the cake. Cats rule at Judith's house. They even jump up on the kitchen counters."

Judith. Hmm. The colleague had a name. And he'd been to her house. "It's possible Judith cleans her counters before she starts to bake, Colin."

Sally cut a wedge and transferred it to a plate. She lifted it to eye level and inspected it carefully. "I don't see any cat hair. The cake looks delicious, though. Come on, give it a try."

She brought a forkful to Colin's mouth. "Mmm, chocolate. Doesn't that smell good?"

Like a reluctant toddler, he accepted the offering. After a few seconds the frown lines on his forehead disappeared.

"Not bad."

Men were suckers for a good chocolate cake. Sally cut a second piece while Colin poured two cups of coffee. "Let's go to the study," he suggested.

They ate their dessert sitting on the sofa overlooking the view from the front window. The river valley was tinged with green now that the poplar trees were in bud. Summer would be here soon.

Sally's attention returned to the room. She focused on a couple of family photographs she'd never noticed before. "Is that your mother?" Something about the woman seemed familiar.

Colin followed the direction of her focus. "Yes.

That was taken last Christmas. The twins belong to my sisters. Cute aren't they?"

One boy and one girl, both with missing front teeth. "They really are. Do they live here in Calgary?"

"Vancouver. My sister moved there after she married. My mother lives there, too, now."

"Did she move there after the divorce?" Edward Foster, Colin's father, was a legend in Calgary's oil and gas circles. The company he'd founded was still going strong. In fact, the current CEO had recently announced the acquisition of several promising new properties.

"Yes. And my dad just moved to Florida with wife number two. A cute redhead about a decade younger than me."

Sally didn't know what to say. "Oh."

"You know, I was an adult when my parents filed for divorce, but it's still weird. It's like I had a family once and now I don't. I haven't seen my dad since Beth's funeral."

"What about your mom and your sister's family?"

"I flew to Vancouver this year for Christmas. But Mom hasn't been the same since Dad remarried. She seems smaller, somehow. She loves the kids, but doesn't have much interest in anything else right now."

He turned to her. "What about your parents? Are they still together?"

"In a manner of speaking, I guess they are. They died not that many years ago. First my father had a massive heart attack. A few months later Mom developed a flu that landed her in the hospital. Within twenty-four hours she was gone."

Sally got up from the sofa and stacked their dirty dishes onto an end table. She noticed Colin had eaten every crumb of his cake.

"I'm sorry," Colin said. "Do you miss them?"

"At times. But we'd grown apart. They didn't like to leave their café in Medicine Hat. And I was busy with my law practice and Lara."

"It happens all too easily, doesn't it?" Colin stood, then reached for the pile of dirty dishes. "Excuse me a minute while I take these to the kitchen."

"Sure." She strolled to his desk where files were neatly piled and organized. The current issue of the *Lawyers Weekly* sat open by the computer. Next to that was a pad of paper...

Sally did a double take when she noticed a date at the top of the page, circled twice: September 3. Lara's birthday.

Beneath that was scrawled "typical 266-day gestation period." Then a column of numbers that she realized were the days of each month counting back from September. At the end of the column, Colin had written December 12, and again he'd circled this date two times.

She realized what this was all about, of course. Colin had been trying to figure out exactly when Lara had been conceived.

"You were right," Colin said, as he strode back into the room. "That cake *was* good. I'm glad I didn't let it go moldy in my—" Noticing her at his desk, he stopped. "What's the matter, Sally? You look—"

Sally held up her hand, motioning him to be silent. What was going on here? Was he pretending to want to date her because he thought he was Lara's father?

And was it possible he really was?

CHAPTER ELEVEN

"I SEE YOU FOUND— I know it must—" Colin shut his mouth. It seemed he was doomed to utter nothing but incomplete sentences for the present. He'd intended to make a joke of his sudden suspicion that he might be Lara's father, mostly because he was so sure it couldn't be true.

But seeing Sally's shocked reaction, he realized laughing this off wasn't going to work.

"Sorry, Sally. I don't know what got into me. I haven't been myself since…well, since Beth died, really. Spending time with you lately got me thinking about the past. And then seeing more of Lara, well, this will sound crazy, but her smile reminded me of my mother. When she was younger."

Sally, frozen, continued to stare at him, her mouth slightly gaping. This wasn't going well. He ought to just shut up. But the words wouldn't stop.

"I don't seriously think that I'm Lara's father. Of course, you would have told me if I was. I was just amusing myself with the possibility. Now I see it was insensitive, to say the least. I *am* sorry, Sally."

At last he ran out of things to say. After a painful pause, Sally finally blinked. She ran a hand over the paper with his calculations. Then she asked him a very peculiar question, in a very peculiar voice.

"What makes you think I would *know* if you were the father?"

"But—wouldn't you?" Colin felt as if the room had suddenly gotten colder. Then he remembered something that afforded him comfort. "We used protection. Every time."

"I always used protection with Neil, too."

Colin frowned. "Are you saying that you're not sure who the father is?" That couldn't be right. But as Sally wrapped her arms around her body, he could see that she looked frightened to death.

"What about the dates, Sally? You can figure it out from those, right?" He picked up the pad of paper and felt the reassuring weight of all those facts in his hands. "Based on an average gestation period of—"

"The key word there is *average*. As any obstetrician will tell you, gestation periods vary from woman to woman."

He didn't want that to be true, but what she said made sense. "Well, the dates have to work within a certain range, right? I mean, give or take a week or two we ought to be able to calculate—"

"Colin, I first slept with Neil less than one week after we were together."

That floored him. "So soon?" He hadn't slept with another woman—Beth—for at least a month.

"Neil swept me off my feet."

Sally said this so dryly he couldn't tell if she was sincere or not. But what did it matter? The issue here wasn't whether Sally had cared about him back then or not. The issue was whether he could possibly be Lara's father.

For the first time, it seemed that he might be. And Colin wasn't sure how he should feel about that.

"Does Neil know that he might not be the father?"

Sally closed her eyes, then turned away from him. After a few moments, he realized she was crying. Oh God. Oh, no. He'd never been good in situations like this.

"Are you okay?" He moved closer and tentatively touched her shoulder. When she didn't pull away, he placed his arm across her back. "It's okay, Sally," he murmured.

But was it? He really didn't have a clue.

"I'm so confused. I always assumed Neil was the father. I mean, you and I were together that one night only."

Yeah, but *three times* that night. Colin decided it would be wise to withhold that clarification for the moment.

"You and I had a one-night stand. Neil and I had a *relationship.* I don't remember our protection ever failing, but if it did—and it must have—surely it would have been when I was with Neil?"

Sally turned her tear-streaked face in his direction, and he longed to reassure her. But heck. This was major shit.

"So previous to now, you've never considered that anyone but Neil could be Lara's father?"

"No. It sounds naive now, but I really didn't. Maybe I had a few inklings of doubt when I first realized I was pregnant. But I never seriously thought…"

"So it is *possible,* even if it's just a remote possibility, that I could be the…biological…father?"

She looked away. "Unlikely. But possible, I guess."

"But—" He was back to truncated sentences. Because not only did he not have a clue about what to say, he also was clueless about how to feel.

"We need to find out the truth," he said finally.

"But that would take a DNA test."

"I've actually done some research on that, too," he confessed.

Sally's eyes widened.

He swallowed and continued. "It isn't that difficult. All we need are saliva samples from me, Lara… and you, too, if you're willing. They can get us the results in seven business days."

She just stared at him.

"I'm moving too fast, right?" He wanted to fold her into his arms, but he could tell she was more comfortable with distance right now. He leaned against the desk and hoped he could make her understand.

"I know it's a long shot. Lara is probably Neil's daughter and nothing will be gained by doing this paternity test. But I'd really like to know for sure."

Sally's eyes narrowed as she backed away from him. "When did you first notice this supposed resemblance between Lara and your mother?"

"A few weeks ago. When I saw her photograph in your family room."

Sally looked away and drew in a deep breath. When she turned to face him again, her expression was completely distant and analytical. "Is that why you asked me out for dinner? Because you thought Lara might be your child?"

"No. My feelings for you have nothing to do with this. Nothing." He could see the distrust in her eyes. "I wasn't planning to bring this up. I wanted our relationship to be on more solid ground first."

Distrust turned to disbelief. "You were planning to just sit on this?"

She made his motives sound deceptive. "Look, Sally. I'm not trying to hurt you."

She opened her mouth, but nothing came out. Finally, she threw her hands to the air. "This is so absurd. I can't believe it."

"So you're against the DNA testing, I take it?"

"DNA testing," she repeated bitterly. "You think it's going to be so simple?"

"Well, it's not complicated. You just swipe a cotton swab inside your mouth…"

"That's simple, all right. And what do you suggest I say to Lara when I'm taking this sample. *Just want to make sure I didn't make a mistake about who your father is, honey.*" Sally shook her head angrily. "I'm sure that will go over really well."

He put a hand to his chin. "I can see this is a little more tricky than I thought."

Sally let out a noisy breath. "Tricky? Colin, you have no idea."

ON THURSDAYS Sally volunteered as a dispute resolutions officer at the courthouse. This Thursday she was mediating between a man and a woman in the process of a divorce.

The proceedings were amazingly civil. Both parties were polite, even kind, to each other. They listened when the other was speaking, and made their decisions with the best interests of the children in mind.

At the end of the session, Sally couldn't help but say, "Are you two sure you want a divorce? You seem to be very compatible."

They laughed at that, but there was a definite tinge of sadness in the man's eyes when he shook her hand goodbye.

He still loves his wife. She squeezed his hand, trying to convey her sympathy and understanding with that one gesture. His brief smile thanked her for her small kindness.

She watched them leave the building together. When they reached the main sidewalk, they separated. The wife turned left; the husband right. Sally felt an overwhelming tenderness for the man. Even though he didn't want to end his marriage, his behavior had been so decent. Not just where his kids were concerned, but his wife, as well.

There are good people out there.

If only she could run into them a little more often.

AT HOME SHE FOUND Lara sitting at the kitchen table, her head bent over a book. She was reading *Memoirs of a Geisha* for her English 10 book report.

"What's for dinner?"

"My day was fine thanks. How was yours?" Sally plopped the grocery bags on the island, pulling out two salmon fillets and a package of baby potatoes. She hoped the lettuce she'd bought on Monday was still fresh. She pulled out the bottom drawer of the fridge, opened the bag and sniffed. Not bad. Only a few leaves had turned brown.

She sorted out the bad stuff, then rinsed the rest and returned it to the fridge so it would be crisp by dinnertime.

"Good book?" She switched on the oven, washed the salmon, then arranged it on a baking sheet.

"Mmm." Lara still hadn't taken her eyes off the page. But suddenly she straightened. "Is this a metaphor, Mom?" She read the passage aloud and when Sally confirmed her diagnosis, picked up a pen to copy it down.

Using her left hand.

Wasn't Colin left-handed, too?

Sally wished she could look at her daughter without searching for signs of her father in her. But that was impossible now. The truth was, Lara didn't look at all like Neil. He always said she'd inherited the Anderson brains. But Sally wasn't exactly a dummy herself and neither was Colin.

There was the elegant nose to fall back on. That was a feature of Lara's that Sally had always attributed to the Anderson side. She moved to the other side of the island to see Lara in profile.

"What are you doing, Mom? You're like, staring at me. Do I have a zit or something?"

"Sorry, Lara. I'm just trying to remember the book I read when I was in grade ten English. I think it was *To Kill a Mockingbird*."

Lara gave her a *who cares* shrug and kept reading.

Sally returned to the stove side of the island. She wrapped the potatoes in foil with a bit of butter and rosemary, then tossed them into the oven.

At least Colin was being decent about the situation. Last night he'd assured her he wasn't going to try to force her to get DNA tests done or anything. Not that he had any legal right to do so. As to moral rights, well, Sally did feel he had some of those.

Oh, why was she in this predicament? It wasn't as if she'd made a habit of sleeping around. She'd only had one lover before Colin—a steady boyfriend from high school whom she'd broken up with in second year. Nice girls like her weren't supposed to be unsure of the paternity of their children.

What if word of this got out into the public? She could just see the headlines. Prospective Queen's Court Judge Embroiled In Paternity Suit. Some enterprising reporter would snap a close-up of Lara. It would make the cover of the *Sun,* along with a provocative headline: Who Is This Child's Father? Her Own Mother Doesn't Know.

Sally groaned.

"Are you sick or something? I'm going to read in my room. Give a shout when dinner's ready."

"I'll do that, Lara." And would you like me to call you when I've figured out who your father is, too?

As soon as Lara had disappeared down the hall, Sally went for the phone.

"I HOPE YOU DON'T MIND, Colin. I had to talk to some-one. I feel like I'm going crazy."

Me, too, Colin wanted to say, but since Sally had made the call, she had dibs on vying for sympathy here.

"I can't believe I went all these years just *assuming*. And now I can't sleep at night for wondering if I might have been wrong. Also, I can't even look at my daughter anymore without—"

She didn't finish that thought, but he understood anyway. She'd be searching Lara's face, trying to find that one bit of irrefutable proof that Lara was Neil's daughter.

Of course, that was what Sally wanted. Assurance that the man she'd married was indeed the father of the child they'd raised together.

He ought to want the same thing. For Sally's sake. And Lara's and Neil's. But he must have a selfish streak in him somewhere. And it was a pretty damn big one. Because the more he stewed this over, the more he found he *liked* the idea of being Lara's father.

Oh, he'd missed out on so much. Just about ev-erything, really. Still, the idea of having a child. It was just—incredibly, amazingly, good.

If he let himself, he could get worked up about the injustice of the situation. Sally should have fig-ured this out before she married Neil. At the very least she should have spoken to both of them and let them know the possibilities.

But he could understand why she'd assumed Neil was the dad. The truth was she'd always considered their encounter a mistake. She'd probably convinced herself it hadn't really happened. Besides, as she'd so logically pointed out, the odds were heavily in favor of Neil.

All this speculation was probably only that. Speculation.

"Don't worry, Sally. I'm not going to tell anyone and neither are you. Neil *is* Lara's father. He's supported her and loved her and looked after her for all these years. That's not going to change."

There was a moment's pause, then Sally's heavy sigh. "You know something, Colin? That makes two decent men in one day for me. It must be some kind of record."

"I'm not that decent. I want something in exchange."

"Let me guess. Does it come with tomato sauce?"

He laughed. "No, it comes in high heels and a pretty black dress. Will you have dinner with me again this weekend? Friday night?"

"I have book club that night. Which reminds me, I've got to read the darn novel."

"How about Saturday? I know it's your weekend with Lara, but I'm betting she has plans."

"She does."

He heard the hesitation in her voice and knew she was struggling with this decision. He waited for her to make up her mind, praying for the right outcome.

"Okay, Colin, yes. I'd love to have dinner on Saturday."

He hung up the phone, puttered around the kitchen, then, when there was nothing more to do, found himself wandering the house.

He felt so strange. Like he'd shed ten pounds and was walking on a spongy new pair of tennis shoes. What the hell was going on?

The answer came in a flash and he realized that he hadn't experienced this emotion since Beth's initial diagnosis, when life—as he'd known it—had changed forever.

Anticipation.

Finally the future was something he could look forward to again.

As for the question of Lara's paternity, he could afford to let the question sit for a while. He had faith in Sally's sense of fair play. Eventually she'd realize that he had a right to know and she'd agree to the DNA testing.

As for what they'd tell Lara when that time came…he had no idea.

CHAPTER TWELVE

NEIL WAS ALMOST POSITIVE Sally had a date lined up for Saturday night. He'd called Lara earlier in the afternoon. His daughter had been painting her nails in preparation for going to the movies with a boy from her ski team.

"I can't talk long, Daddy. I still have to apply the top coat. Then Mom wants me to take Armani for a long walk because he's going to be alone tonight."

Neil already knew Lara had a date. He wasn't thrilled about the fact that his daughter was now old enough to go out with boys. But he'd grown to accept the fact. Sally was another matter.

"Why can't your mother take him for a walk?"

"She's getting her hair done. Anyway, Armani is my responsibility, too. Mom already does way more than her share."

Neil hated it when Lara stuck up for her mother. He hated even more the way Lara would suddenly become quiet whenever he introduced Sally into the conversation.

When his daughter was younger, chatty and un-guarded, it had been so much easier to keep tabs on his former wife. Now Lara was cautious when dis-cussing her mother with him. He knew she would not tell him why Sally wouldn't be home tonight un-less he asked. And maybe not even then.

So, he'd have to find another way. Neil picked up the phone and canceled his plans with the woman he'd being seeing recently. She sounded disap-pointed, but he didn't care. If she turned him down the next time he asked her out, he'd quickly find an-other willing woman to take her place.

Around six o'clock he went into the garage and slipped into his second vehicle. He rarely drove the inconspicuous Toyota and knew Sally wouldn't think of him if she happened to see the car in her neighbor-hood.

He drove to Elbow Valley and found a good spot to sit and wait. He had a copy of the newspaper and a large take-out coffee to occupy him while he waited to see what would happen.

Just before seven, Chris showed up for Lara. Neil watched his beautiful daughter come running out of the house, and felt a familiar swell of pride at the sight of her. Though her dating was a tough thing to get used to, he was glad that she was popular with her peers.

Just like her old man, he thought to himself.

Though his popularity had definitely been higher with the girls than the boys his own age.

About a half hour after Chris drove off with Lara, a second vehicle pulled up in front of Sally's house. Neil recognized the SUV right away. It was the same one from a few weeks ago. The Friday night that he and Sally had had their…disagreement.

He pulled out a pair of binoculars, anxious to get a good look at the driver when he stepped out of the car. But it turned out he didn't need them. He recognized the man right away.

Colin Foster.

Talk about a blast from the past. They'd all gone to law school together and Colin had married Sally's best friend. Back when Neil and Sally had been married, they'd seen a fair amount of the Fosters.

After the divorce, all that had changed. Colin was friendly enough when his path crossed with Neil's in the legal community. But the few times he'd seen Beth, she'd given him the cold shoulder.

Of course, Beth was dead now. Neil had seen the obituary last autumn. So what was going on between Colin and Sally now? Surely nothing romantic…?

Sally opened the front door and stepped outside. Neil remembered Lara saying her mother had an appointment with the hairdresser today. Well, the results were terrific. At work and when in court, Sally almost always wore her hair back, but tonight it was long and softly curled. She was all dressed up, too, with high heels that made the most of her sexy legs.

Neil closed his eyes and imagined Sally was getting into the car with him. He could almost smell her perfume wafting in the air, could almost hear the sound of her deep-throated laughter, so at odds with her delicate appearance.

He remembered when her eyes had sparkled at the sight of him. Now they almost always narrowed with a watchful distrust. She was so ungrateful. So selfish. All she cared about was her own career, her own love life, while he had always acted with nothing but their family's best interests at heart.

He opened his eyes again and watched Sally lock the front door. He smiled at the ineffectual gesture. Wouldn't Sally flip if she guessed he had a key? There were a lot of things about him that she had absolutely no clue about.

Through his open car window he heard her laugh at something Foster said and his fists clenched. Then she slipped into the front passenger seat of the SUV. Foster shut her door before loping to the driver side.

He sure looked eager, that son of a bitch. Eager to take off with a woman he had absolutely no right to even think of touching.

Adrenaline, fueled by a potent mixture of anger and jealousy, raced through Neil's veins. Something was going on between these two, no doubt about it. Clearly they were going out on a date.

Were they sleeping together, too?

Anger quickly turned to rage, and Neil gripped the steering wheel tighter and tighter. There were aspects of being divorced that he'd become resigned to over time. Living in separate houses. Sharing access to Lara.

But what he could not abide, could never abide, was the thought of Sally in another man's arms. She was the mother of his child. She ought to be keeping herself pure for that reason, if no other.

As they drove away, Neil hesitated for seconds only. Then he started the Toyota and followed.

THEY WERE TALKING less and less about Beth these days. Sally took a sip of her water. She had a clear view out the restaurant window and could see Colin pacing up and down the sidewalk as he dealt with an emergency call he'd received a moment ago. She didn't resent the interruption to their evening; in a way she welcomed it.

She needed the opportunity to catch her breath. Colin was having that effect on her a lot lately. And it worried her. Though she'd dated a little, she hadn't had a serious romantic relationship since her divorce.

About eight years ago she'd started seeing an

older man on a regular basis. He was a high-profile cabinet minister with the Alberta government and they'd purposefully kept their relationship low-key at first.

But somehow Neil had discovered what was going on. He'd left her a nasty message on her voice mail at work and the next day when Sally was on her way to court she'd found the front end of her car completely caved in. She'd been late for court and the cops had never found the vehicle or the driver who was responsible for the hit-and-run accident.

She'd known it was Neil.

A couple years later a similar mishap occurred when she began to date a fellow attorney at the office. Important documentation for one of her cases had gone missing. When she'd stopped seeing the guy, the file was miraculously returned.

"Could it have been here on your desk all this time?" her bemused assistant had asked.

But again, Sally had known Neil was responsible.

She'd installed a separate lock for her office, purchased a security system for her home. And yet, she continued to live in apprehension, never knowing when Neil might try to make her life miserable again.

Though she'd often complained to Beth about Neil, she hadn't confessed these more bizarre acts of interference. Beth would have expected her to take action. She would not have understood that it was easier to let Neil think he was successfully controlling her life than to put up a fight where Lara would be the real loser.

Sally didn't have time for romantic entanglements, anyway. Her devotion to her career as well as Lara left very little free time.

Realistically speaking, when could she squeeze time into her day planner for a man?

And yet, she had no problem finding time for Colin.

She felt her pulse speed up as he returned to their table.

"Sorry about that," Colin said, slipping into his seat. "We have a high-profile case coming up next week. One of my staff members is working late on it tonight and needed my opinion on something."

"What's the case, Colin? Can you talk about it?"

"Does the name Alderman Victor Exshaw ring any bells?"

"You're kidding." Of course she was familiar with the facts. They'd been dominating the local press for weeks. While attending a charitable function at the Glenbow Museum, Alderman Exshaw had allegedly pocketed a beautiful carving from a display of Inuit artifacts.

"Did he really do it?"

"That's our case." Colin leaned back in his seat as their coffees were served. "We have a witness and fingerprint evidence. Unfortunately, the video-camera footage is useless because someone was blocking that particular display case when the crime occurred."

"Accidentally, or on purpose?"

"I like the way you think. On purpose, is my guess. It can't be a coincidence that the woman blocking the scene was the alderman's girlfriend. Mrs. Exshaw isn't going to be too pleased if that fact comes out in court."

"I should say not." Sally took the crispy biscotti from the side of her cup and dipped it into the frothy cappuccino. They'd talked about work quite a bit tonight. Also about travel, the health-care system and hockey.

In the beginning Beth had been the focus of all of her and Colin's conversations. But tonight her name hadn't come up even once.

Should she feel guilty about that?

Did Colin?

Judging by his appearance at the moment, she'd have to say no. He'd smiled quite a lot tonight, and he was smiling now. He reached across the table to touch her hand.

"I'm enjoying this very much, Sally."

So was she. Too much. A movement from the street drew her eye to the window in time to see a dark-haired man walk by.

For a second she thought it was Neil. He'd been about the right size, the right age... But surely Neil had better things to do on a Saturday night than skulk around his ex-wife and her date.

She was really getting paranoid here.

THOUGH SALLY WAS tempted to accept Colin's offer of a nightcap at his house, she declined. She wanted to be home well before Lara's curfew at midnight. Colin walked her to the door and unlocked it for her.

"Are you sure you won't change your mind?"

He was holding her close as he asked the question, putting her at unfair disadvantage. For one sweet moment she let her head sink against his chest. She loved the way his arms warmly enveloped her in response.

"It looks awfully dark and lonely in there." Colin bent his head to whisper these words into her ear.

"You're leading the witness, Counselor."

"I'm trying, Your Honor. But she won't follow."

"I *want* to follow. But I have to do my anxious-parent routine now. You know, where I count the minutes before midnight and pace in front of the living-room window watching for lights in the drive-way."

"Sounds grueling. How about one kiss before I go?"

It seemed like such a small request. One that Sally would normally have been only pleased to fulfill. But suddenly she felt awkward and exposed standing on her front porch for all to see.

For *Neil* to see.

She'd been spooked since she'd imagined she'd seen her ex outside the restaurant. On the way home, she kept checking over her shoulder for a glimpse of his green Jaguar. Now, she scanned the street and saw nothing but a dark-colored Toyota parked several houses away.

She put her hands on Colin's chest and kept the kiss to one short, sweet peck.

"That's it?"

His mouth lingered near hers and she had to close her eyes and pull in a deep breath in order to find the strength to break away.

"Thanks for a wonderful evening, Colin."

He gave in with a rueful smile. "I'm missing you already, Sally Stowe. And I haven't even left you yet."

She almost gave in then and let him inside. But she knew the way time seemed to evaporate when she was with Colin. She didn't want Lara to come home from her date to find her mother entertaining a man.

Besides, she couldn't shake the irrational feeling that Neil could somehow see what she was doing.

Colin seemed to sense the direction of her thoughts. "You're not brushing me off because of Lara, are you? This is about Neil again."

She wanted to say no. Instead, she shrugged. "Please be patient, Colin. It won't be much longer."

"I guess there's no point in me asking when we can see each other?"

Again she shrugged. "I'll call you."

Colin gave a brisk nod. "I get the picture."

No, you don't! As he strode for his car, Sally longed to call him back. It wasn't often that life offered you a second chance at something you really wanted. Now she and Colin had that chance, and she was letting it slip away.

Several times Sally almost ran out to the street to stop him. But saner instincts kept her where she was. She couldn't forget the other problem between her and Colin. The problem of her daughter's paternity. The more she saw of Colin, the sooner she'd have to deal with that bombshell. At present, she simply preferred not to think about it.

Great coping strategy, Sally.

Once the taillights of Colin's SUV were out of sight, Sally locked up, leaving the outdoor lights on for Lara. She drifted to the kitchen to make herself a cup of herbal tea. Her plan was to sit in the chair by the front window, listen to a little Diana Krall, and wait for Lara.

But when she flicked on the kitchen lights, she saw a foreign object on the floor by the island. She went to investigate. It was a rock about the size of a baseball.

How in the world?

Then she felt the cool spring breeze at her ankles and her focus shot over to the window. One of the mullioned panes had been shattered. Tiny shards of glass glinted like silver on the floor.

Suddenly she had an awful feeling that she wasn't alone in the house. She whirled around but saw nothing. No one. Armani started whining in the laundry room and she realized she'd forgotten all about him. He'd need to go outside, but she didn't dare release him from the laundry room until she'd cleaned up this glass.

She put a hand to her chest and felt the racing of her heart. Could an intruder be in her house? Logic told her: no way. The window was too tiny for anyone to have gained access that way. And she'd left the house completely locked, according to the green lights on her activated security system.

Leaning against the edge of the island, she took a few deep, calming breaths. Should she call the police? Colin would be here in a flash if she phoned and told him what had happened. But this was probably an act of adolescent vandalism. She recalled the two preteen boys who lived several houses back and who'd recently been expelled from school for defacing school property. Probably this was their handiwork.

When her initial panic had subsided, she went to the closet and pulled out rubber gloves, a dustpan and broom. She picked up the bigger chunks of glass by hand, then swept the smaller shards into a pile that she scooped into the garbage. Carefully she cleared the remaining glass from the window frame, then used masking tape and clear plastic to block the wind.

Tomorrow she'd call to have this repaired. One little pane of glass wouldn't be that expensive. As more time passed she was glad she hadn't overreacted and reported the misdemeanor to the police. This was not a big deal.

She'd just let Armani out to the yard, when she heard the sound of a vehicle outside. Sally fought the desire to run and open the front door. Instead, she put the kettle on and pulled out two bags of tea. Peppermint for her, mango spice for Lara.

By the time her daughter made her way into the house, the two cups of tea were ready.

"Hi Mom! Are you home?"

"In the kitchen."

Lara entered the room looking pleased. The date must have gone well. She slid up on the bar stool next to Sally and wrapped her hands around the warm mug.

"Did you have a good time?"

Lara smiled and nodded. "I did."

"I'm glad, hon. Chris seems like a nice guy."

"It was weird at first. Being with him without the rest of the gang from the ski team."

"I guess it would be."

"But we ended up finding lots of things to talk about."

Talk. That was good. "Where did you go for pizza?"

"To this totally cool place in Marda Loop. They had all sorts of weird toppings, but Chris and I both like pepperoni and cheese best."

Sally smiled to herself. Ah, the sophisticated teenage palate.

"And what movie did you end up seeing?"

"Something dumb. I don't even remember the title. We left halfway through and went for a walk instead."

Sally felt a jolt of alarm. "You did? Where?"

"Battalion Park."

The park was on a steep hill, north of the movie plaza. Regiment numbers from World War I were outlined in white rock for the city to see. Next to the numbers, a long wooden staircase allowed pedestrians to travel from Signal Hill down to the Westside shopping center below. Sally tried not to picture two teenagers necking on the convenient wooden landing in the middle of the stairs.

Or worse, two teenagers doing more than just necking in the back seat of Chris's car…

"Chill, Mom. It was perfectly safe at the park. And we didn't do what I know you're worrying we might have done. This was our first real date."

Sally took a sip of tea. "I trust you, Lara."

She snorted. "Right. That's what Dad always says, too. Right before he gives me the hour lecture on not growing up too fast, savoring my youth, and protecting my health."

Sally gave a prayer of thanks that Neil's head was screwed on right when it came to their daughter.

"He's right, you know."

"At least you two agree about something."

Sally heard hidden depths in that comment. How much did the tension between her and Neil bother Lara? Perhaps more, now that she was older.

"I'm sorry your father and I don't get along as well as we should. I know it's hard for you."

She'd surprised her daughter by broaching a subject she usually avoided. For a moment Lara said nothing. Then she sniffed. "I hate the way he talks to you."

She'd been naive to hope Neil's sarcastic digs went unnoticed by their daughter. Sally shook her head sadly.

"He treats you like…dirt. And you never stand up to him! You just go all quiet and cold."

"But—" Sally stopped, surprised that Lara saw the situation that way. She'd always refused to stoop to Neil's level. But instead of seeing her mother as morally superior, Lara saw her as a wimp. "Would you rather we fought and yelled every time we saw each other?"

"Of course not. But you…oh, I don't know." Lara slipped off the stool. "Can I finish my tea in my room?"

Sally wanted to say, *We're not finished here.* But Lara was tired. And there were tears in her eyes. "Go right ahead, hon." Sally reached over to give her a hug. "I love you, Lara."

"I love you too, Mom."

Sally listened to the reassuring sound of her daughter's footsteps going down the hall to her room. The bedroom door closed then all was silent again.

Sally let her shoulders sink and her head droop forward. Her little girl had grown up so fast. All too often she had no idea what was going on in her head. Like this latest bombshell. She couldn't believe that Lara saw her as weak.

Exhausted, Sally picked up her mug and headed for the dishwasher. As she rounded the island, she stubbed her toe on something hard.

"Darn!"

She grabbed her toe and squeezed. God, how could one small body part hurt this much? She waited for the pain to subside, then looked down to see what she'd kicked.

It was the rock. That stupid, damn rock. Suddenly she was angry. She picked it up, deciding that tomorrow she would go and talk to those boys. She couldn't let them get away with destroying her property and—

Wait. Something had been scratched into the stone. Sally held it up to the light and there they were, five letters that must have been chiseled with a nail, or a similar sharp object.

The five letters spelled *bitch*.

And at that moment Sally knew this rock hadn't been thrown by vandals. Not the boys down the street or any other kids in the neighborhood.

This was Neil's handiwork.

Something that had been buried deep inside of her for many, many years began to bubble up. As she stood motionless in her kitchen, Sally felt the emotion push its way through her veins until her entire body pulsed with its power.

Anger. Pure, fearless anger.

With the anger, came a startling insight. Lara was right to consider her a coward. When she avoided discussing certain subjects, or arranged her love life to suit Neil's specifications, wasn't that exactly what she was being?

She'd convinced herself that ugly scenes were to be avoided at any price. But was that for Lara's sake?

Or for her own?

Always turning the other cheek may have worked in biblical times, but it was destroying her spirit and possibly a piece of Lara's, too.

Well, no longer. Starting immediately, she wasn't putting up with Neil's bullshit any longer.

CHAPTER THIRTEEN

BY MONDAY MORNING Sally's fury hadn't cooled. It had however, with hours of reflection, become focused. She was adopting a new approach with her ex-husband. She didn't care about the judicial appointment specifically or about what other people might think or say in general. Enough was enough.

First, she called Colin. She was still a little conflicted about their relationship. She hated feeling that she was betraying her best friend and she definitely didn't want to deal with the possibility that he could be Lara's father.

But she'd hardly slept last night for thinking about the wounded look in his eyes as he'd left. Whatever problems she and Colin had to deal with, her ex-husband was no longer going to be one of them.

At first Colin's pleasure at hearing her voice seemed tepid at best.

"Sally? I didn't think I'd hear from you so soon."

"You underestimate your powers, Counselor."

He chuckled. Then the line was silent. "What about Neil?"

"Forget him. I was foolish to think his opinion counted for anything. All that matters is that I'd like to see you again, and soon. I'm hoping you feel the same way?"

Colin kept her waiting a second, then said, "The Flames are playing at home and I have two tickets. I could probably get my hands on a third. Would you and Lara like to join me?"

"It's Neil's weekend, so Lara can't. But I'd love to come."

"And you're sure you're not worried if Neil hears that we're seeing each other?"

"I've been foolish to even care. We've been divorced more than thirteen years." And she saw now, so clearly, that she should have stood up to him years ago. The first time he'd pulled one of his mean, adolescent stunts.

"I'm glad. 'Cause frankly I've been a little worried about the degree of control he has over you."

"That's *had,* not *has.* I'm not putting up with his crap anymore, Colin. I had a talk with Lara on Saturday night when she came home from her date and I was really startled to see the situation from her point of view. I thought I was keeping the peace for her sake, I thought I was being strong. But she had this really sad picture of me as a victim."

Which was the *last* kind of role model she wanted to be for her daughter.

"You've been in a tough situation."

He was just making excuses for her. Why had she never seen any of this clearly before? Sally doodled vicious black spirals on the notepad by her phone.

"The situation is changing. Starting today."

Colin's tone turned cautious. "Well, be careful. Neil may not be too pleased with you abandoning the status quo. If you need me to act as buffer…"

"That's kind of you to offer." But she would handle this on her own. She *had* to.

"He hurt you once. I'm terrified that he might do it again."

"I'll be careful," she promised. After setting a time for their date on Saturday, Sally hung up the phone with a renewed sense of purpose. She was doing the right thing.

She placed a second call, this one to the front desk receptionist. "Evelyn, do we have a cardboard box big enough for a baseball?"

"Is this for a gift?"

"I guess you could call it that."

"Just a minute, Ms. Stowe."

Five minutes later Evelyn set a six-inch square box on her desk, along with bubble wrap and packing tape.

"Want me to take care of it for you?" the young woman offered helpfully.

"No, thanks." She waited until Evelyn had left, then put on a pair of household cleaning gloves she'd brought from home. From her briefcase, she removed the stone that had crashed through her window and wiped it clean before wrapping it in the packing material, then putting it into the box.

Quickly she printed off a generic label with Neil's work address. Another that said "private and confidential." When she was done, she examined the package carefully. She knew a private courier company whose owner owed her a few favors. He would deliver this without any telltale return address.

In no way could this package be traced back to her.

But Neil would sure know who had sent it.

AFTER COURT on Tuesday, Neil's curiosity was roused by a strange-shaped package sitting on his desk at the office. He also had a phone message from his mother. After finding out about Sally's new boyfriend, he'd been too upset to make his usual filial Sunday-morning phone call.

And he was still too stressed to deal with his mother now. He crumpled the phone message and tossed it into the garbage. Then he turned to the package.

"Where did this come from?" he asked the new receptionist who'd been hovering in the hallway. He didn't know her name, but he wondered if they were hiring straight from high school now. This girl seemed barely older than Lara to him. And was there a facial feature she hadn't pierced? Thank God, Lara didn't go for that nonsense.

The receptionist stepped into his office. "Oh, that. It was delivered by afternoon courier."

"There must have been a return address."

"I couldn't see one, sir."

He shook his head, weary of the endless incompetence he seemed to encounter wherever he went. In court today, he'd been dismayed to discover that his staff had screwed up on the medical history of the defendant. He hated looking like an idiot in front of a judge.

He hoped the junior lawyers he'd reamed out an hour ago were working hard to rectify their ineptitude. But he no longer held out high hopes for this particular angle of his defense. He'd have to come up with something else.

As he pondered the various legal arguments open to him, his fingers worked to tear away tape from the package. He balled the sticky mass and tossed it into the trash. Then he opened the box.

The item was heavy and probably fragile, since it had been wrapped with care. He peeled back the bubble wrap and for a second his mind went completely blank.

A rock?

And then it hit him. This was *the* rock. He could

see the word he'd scratched into it with his Phillips screwdriver.

Sally must have sent this to him.

Surprise was quickly engulfed by anger. So the bitch was trying to assert herself? God, he should have shoved her harder when he'd had the chance. Really taught her a lesson.

His right hand clenched over the stone as he imagined the pleasure of eliminating—once and for all—the haughty expression from Sally's porcelain doll face. With attitude like hers, she should have been born into the royal family.

But she was just a kid from small-town Alberta. Nothing until she'd married him. What right did she have to look at him with such superiority in her eyes? He'd graduated with marks just as high as hers. And he'd progressed in their profession of choice even faster than she had.

If anyone deserved to be a judge… Not that he was willing to give up his current salary for the honor. Still, he hated the idea that Sally might be viewed, by some, to hold a position higher than his.

God, what if he ever had to try a case in her court?

He gripped the rock tighter, imagined hurling it at her face, seeing her crumple at his feet. He'd give anything to reduce her to begging him for mercy. To finally admit that he was the strong one. And that she needed him.

Instead, she was dating another man. Colin Foster of all people. Even in law school Neil had never trusted him. Colin had an annoying habit of making his schoolmates look like fools, then laughing everything off, like it was one big joke.

The phone rang and Neil chose to ignore it. He wasn't in the mood to speak to anyone right now. But then the multipierced receptionist poked her damn head back into his office.

"Your ex-wife is on line two."

Sally? He grabbed for the receiver. Checked his initial impulse to growl. He couldn't let her know how much she was getting to him. He leaned back into his chair and reminded himself that he was the one who called the shots in this relationship.

"Well, Sal," he drawled. "What a pleasure. You so rarely call."

"I'm glad you consider talking to me a pleasure. You may not by the time I'm through."

Threats? From Sally? How intriguing. He placed the rock she'd sent him carefully down on the corner of his desk. "So how can I help you, Sal?"

She almost choked at that.

"I don't have all day," he pressed. "What's this about?"

"That bathing suit you bought Lara is much too skimpy."

That's what had her so upset? The bathing suit?

At the store, Lara had wanted it so badly he hadn't had the heart to say no. But actually he agreed with Sally on this. He'd seen the way the guys ogled his daughter at the hot-tub party and it had made him crazy.

"She picked it out. Not me."

"I know she chose the suit, Neil. The point is, you should have said no."

"But I didn't. So what do you want to do about it?"

"I'm going to insist she put it into our donation pile for Community Living."

Sally gets to be the bad guy. Lara no longer wears the too-skimpy suit. Worked for him. "Fine."

He heard Sally draw a deep breath and that made him smile. She wasn't as cool and collected as she'd like him to believe.

"And about the car…"

"Now what? God, Sal, I have work to do."

"This is important. Lara told me you were planning on buying her a new convertible once she has her driver's license."

"Yeah? So what?"

"She's just sixteen! I don't approve of giving such an extravagant gift at that age. I was thinking of letting her use my car—"

"That granny car for Lara?" He hooted. "Look, Sal, you can drive whatever you want. I'm getting

Lara the BMW convertible. Now, if that's all you called me about…"

"It isn't," Sally said quickly.

He waited a second, then, "Well…?"

"Has the courier been by today, Neil?"

He seized the rock again and smoothed his thumb over the letters he'd carved so crudely. Never had they seemed to apply more appropriately than right now. "As a matter of fact, I did receive something rather puzzling. No return address, but I thought it might be from you."

"Puzzling? Give me a break. I know you threw that rock through my window Saturday night."

"Pardon me? I don't think you have your facts straight, Counselor."

Her voice chilled. "The facts couldn't be more clear."

"If you say so." Actually, he was glad she knew it was him. He'd been afraid she might write the incident off as simple vandalism. He hoped she also knew that he was capable of much, much worse.

"I'm calling the police next time. If you do something like that again, if you damage my possessions or hurt me in *any* way, I'm filing charges. Consider yourself warned."

He snapped upright, unable to believe what he was hearing. The bitch. The *bitch*. Who did she think she was? "Are you hallucinating, Sally? What cop is going to believe that I snuck around in the dark hours just for the pleasure—and I admit it would be a pleasure—of throwing a rock in your kitchen window?"

There was a pause, and he immediately saw his mistake.

"Kitchen, Neil?"

Damn it! "Whatever," he said with feigned boredom.

"For years you've controlled my life with your adolescent antics. But as of today, that's all changing."

Oh, really? Neil curled his fingers, imagining they were around her skinny little neck. "I still have no idea what you're talking about."

She ignored that. "Consider yourself warned," she said. And then she hung up.

Neil fought the urge to hurl the phone—and the rock—across the room. That bitch thought she could order him around, did she? She thought she was suddenly going to take control of their relationship and of her life.

Well, he'd show her. He'd sure as hell show her. And he'd show that arrogant boyfriend of hers, too. In fact, he already had.

Neil took a set of keys from his suit jacket pocket and unlocked the bottom drawer of his desk. Sunday afternoon he'd spent some time following the crown prosecutor. Colin Foster was a careless man, in the habit of taking home important papers and leaving his back door unlocked.

Neil picked up the file he'd managed to remove from Foster's desk. He flipped through the private investigator reports establishing a romantic link between Alderman Exshaw and a pretty young thing who'd worked on his campaign.

How this information fit into the prosecutor's case, Neil wasn't sure. But his gut told him that it was important. And that Foster would flip when he discovered this file missing.

Neil smiled. Playing with Colin Foster's mind was going to be fun.

But he had other games to consider now, too. Sally thought she could start laying down the law…well, he'd show her.

Neil moved the crown prosecutor's file to his briefcase, then dug once more through his bottom drawer. He had all sorts of miscellaneous information in here, including a copy of Sally's e-mail address book.

There'd been one client he'd seen mentioned in the news lately who might provide just the opportunity he needed. Neil scrolled through the list of contacts, then stopped when he found the person he'd been looking for.

Along with the name was an e-mail address, a work number and a cell-phone number. He tried the cell phone and hit pay dirt right away.

He introduced himself and explained his mission succinctly. "I know that you're in trouble with your ex-wife and her lawyer right now and I'm pretty sure I can help you."

He listened to some bluster, then cut back in.

"Totally unfair. I agree with you one-hundred percent. And like I said before, I think I can see a way out of your current situation."

The guy sounded unsure. "I don't have much money."

"It won't cost you a thing," Neil assured the man. "In fact, our self-interests happen to be aligned in this case. So much so that you may actually make a little money out of this."

"Really? What did you say your name was?"

Neil smiled at the man's quick change in tone. Now he really had the guy's attention.

"Never mind names. We'll leave that for our first meeting. How about tomorrow?"

The man suggested lunch.

"Good idea. But let's not go downtown." Neil mentioned an out-of-the-way diner on Sixteenth Avenue. "Noon tomorrow? That sounds perfect."

As soon as he'd disconnected from the call, Neil reached for his electronic organizer. Under Wednesday, he jotted down "lunch with R.M."

This was going to be so damn easy it wasn't funny.

CHAPTER FOURTEEN

ON FRIDAY AFTERNOON Sally had just picked Lara up from school and was driving down Sixty-ninth, when her cell phone rang. She didn't answer, knowing the call would go to her voice mail.

"How was your day, hon?"

Lara grumbled about an unexpected science quiz. They'd marked the papers at school and she'd earned just below eighty. While Lara affected not to care about her grades when she was around her friends, Sally knew she was never satisfied with less than an A.

"Pop quizzes are only a small percentage of your final grade," she reminded Lara. "Besides, a seventy-nine is still a good mark."

Lara crossed her arms and humphed.

Sally fought back a smile. She knew Lara wouldn't appreciate hearing how cute she looked right now. With that pouty expression and dressed in the school's required plaid skirt, long socks and white blouse, she reminded Sally of the little girl who'd once wanted her mom to braid her hair every morning.

Now, Lara wouldn't let Sally anywhere near her carefully layered shoulder-length hair.

The phone started ringing again. This time Lara checked the display. "It's Pam, Mom."

Usually she avoided business conversations in the car, period. But in this case… "Do you mind if I take it?"

"Sure, no problem."

Sally pulled into an empty church parking lot. "What's up, Pam?"

"Rick's really done it this time, Sally. I think we finally pushed him over the edge."

Sally rolled her eyes for Lara's benefit. "What did he do now?"

"I received a letter today by Priority Courier. You'll never believe what was inside."

She was really curious now. "So tell me already."

"You know what? I think you'll have to see this to believe it. Why don't you and Lara come over for pizza?"

"Lara can't. Her father's picking her up in about an hour."

"Just you, then."

"Okay. Shall I bring a bottle of wine?" She thought about Rick's last stunt. "Or maybe two?"

"One will be enough. But hurry. This is the last thing either of us ever would have expected."

PAM WAS PULLING two pizzas out of the oven when Sally arrived almost an hour later.

"Sorry they're homemade," she said. "But it's so much cheaper and the kids seem to like them okay."

"Pam, you're the only person I know who would apologize for serving homemade. Those look delicious. And I'm sure they're much healthier. I did bring some wine. Should I open the bottle?"

"Sure. The corkscrew is in there." Pam pointed. "Wash your hands, kids, then come and sit down."

The four of them settled around a small pine kitchen table. Tabby was in a booster seat, Samuel sat on his knees. Besides the pizza, there were glasses of milk for the kids and a bowl of mini carrots at the center of the table for everyone to share.

"I should have made a proper salad."

"Stop apologizing! This is just great."

The kids certainly thought so. They finished their dinners in record time. Remembering how Lara would dawdle over a meal she didn't like when she was younger, Sally understood that was the truest compliment of all.

Samuel asked if they could watch TV and Pam agreed to put on a video. "Just one and then it's bath time."

They left the two children sitting side by side on the sofa. Back in the kitchen, Pam washed dishes while Sally swept the floor. Toddlers might be cute, but they sure were messy eaters.

Once the kitchen was in order, Sally finally felt it was time to ask. "The suspense is killing me, Pam. What did Rick do?" She hadn't noticed any damage to the front of the house when she'd driven up. And Pam's car had looked okay, as well.

"Look at this." Pam went to the closet and grabbed her purse. She took out a rectangular piece of paper and passed it to Sally.

"It's a check." Sally looked closer. "It's from Rick and it's for…"

"Four months of child support. *Plus* interest. Can you believe it?"

It shouldn't have been such a shock, but Pam was right. It was. Sally glanced at the name of the bank and the address. The check certainly appeared legit.

"I hope it doesn't bounce."

"I have a feeling it won't. It came with a note."

Pam gave her a sheet of paper. On it, Rick wrote that he was sorry about the past and that he intended to make a clean start. He was going to sell his land and go back to work. From now on he'd make his support payments on the first of the month, as agreed.

Sally returned the letter to Pam. This was such

great news. She was surprised, yes, but mostly so happy for Pam and the kids. "Amazing." She didn't know what else to say.

Pam nodded, then smiled wryly at Sally. "I guess I won't be needing so much of your time from now on."

"Maybe not as a client. But as friends?"

Pam squeezed her arm. "Always."

FINALLY SALLY'S CRAZY WEEK was over and the long-anticipated Saturday night arrived. She wore a red Flames jersey over blue jeans for her date with Colin. Five minutes before the agreed time, he rang the doorbell.

When had she last looked forward to an evening this much? She couldn't remember.

She opened the door then planted her hands on her hips. "Do you have any idea how wonderful it is to see you?"

"None whatsoever. But I do know it's absolutely terrific to see you."

Colin had on a Flames jersey, too, as would most of the other hockey fans. Tonight the Saddledome would be a crimson sea of cheering fans.

They bought hot dogs at the game, nachos drenched in melted cheese and chased the junk food down with long drinks of cool, foaming beer.

Even though the Flames ended up losing, Sally

and Colin both came home happy, feeling they'd had a great night out.

"Closing arguments at my place or yours?" Colin asked on the drive home.

"Mine. But don't you mean *statements?*" Then she laughed. No, he'd meant arguments, only she wondered if he'd noticed how much they seemed to agree these days.

In her kitchen she frothed milk for the espressos. While she waited for the steam to build, she pressed the playback button on her answering machine.

"First message," said the recorded voice, followed by a good ten seconds of silence. Only, was that heavy breathing she could hear in the background?

The call ended, and before she could hit the erase button, Colin leaned over to play the message again. He was standing next to her as they listened—more intently this time.

"Neil?" His gray eyes were troubled.

She shrugged. Of course it was possible. Maybe even probable.

"I've been waiting for the right time to ask how things went with him this week."

"Let's sit down, first," Sally said.

"Is it that bad?"

They went to the family room with their coffees. Sally put her feet up and Colin sat next to her.

"Let me backtrack a little. On Saturday night,

after you dropped me home from our dinner, I found a rock in the kitchen and a broken window." She told him about the word she'd found carved into the stone and her assumption that Neil had been responsible.

"Why, that—"

Sally calmed him with a touch on his arm.

"What a moronic stunt. You're sure it was Neil?"

This was what had worried Sally from the beginning. Neil didn't seem like the kind of person to behave so boorishly. Now that she'd decided it was time to blow the whistle, was anyone going to believe her?

Colin seemed to sense her qualms. "Sally, I'm not doubting you. Just thinking like a lawyer."

"I know. But that's what makes this so hard. I don't have any evidence. My gut told me Neil was responsible, so I packaged the rock and couriered it right back to him."

"You didn't?" Colin laughed long and hard over that.

"Then I called him and gave notice that I'd go straight to the police if there was any more trouble. Thanks to that rock, he knows I mean it."

"Good for you." He was silent, thinking. Then, "It won't be easy, will it? Obviously Neil is going to deny pushing you in the kitchen that day and throwing that rock at your window."

"Not easy, no." She thought back to her conversation with Lara last weekend. "But I should have done this much sooner. I also wish I hadn't been so negligent about documenting the incidents over the years."

She should have taken pictures every time he'd damaged something. Made careful note of the specific dates and times of each incident. As a lawyer, she had no excuse not to have done these things. No excuse, except that she'd been so sure she could keep the situation under control if she just stayed calm and pretended not to notice what he was doing to her.

"Well, I can witness the shape you were in that night," Colin said. "Plus there'll be records from the emergency room."

"Yes. Hopefully we won't need any of that."

"Do you think there's a chance Neil will back off?"

"After all these years of feeling he's been controlling me?" She shook her head. "I wish I could say yes, but no, probably not." She set her coffee cup down on the table. "I'm so sick of living with his shadow lingering over my life."

"Those days are definitely over." Colin took her hands in his. "I'm glad you've decided to stand up to him, but you're not doing it alone. I'm going to help you with this. You know that, right?"

For a moment she was tempted to lay her head on

his shoulder and let him tell her everything was going to be fine. But his protective words, though they filled her with warmth, gave her more reason to worry.

"If Neil finds out you're seeing me, he may try to hurt you, too."

An expression flitted across Colin's face, too brief for her to identify. Then he was her strong protector again.

"I'm a big boy, Sally. I'll look after myself."

She looked at him closely. In that split second, he'd given himself away. "Something's already happened, hasn't it?"

When Colin tried to deny it, she pushed harder.

"Please don't hide anything from me, Colin. I couldn't stand it if you did that."

He sighed. "I didn't want to worry you. But you're right. One of the files for the Exshaw case is missing. I may have misplaced it, but—"

"Neil stole it."

Colin shrugged. "The last time I saw the folder, it was on my desk at home. Then I went out to pick up some takeout for dinner and when I came back…" He held up his arms to indicate the file was gone.

"Neil stole it," Sally repeated. There was no doubt in her mind, and she could tell Colin thought the same thing. "I was so worried something like this would happen. I should have warned you to be more careful."

"Well, I am locking up more regularly now," Colin admitted.

"But what about the missing file? Did it contain anything important?" The Exshaw case had been front-page news all week.

"Yes, but it was all replaceable. I don't think Neil was trying to sabotage my case. He was just letting me know that he's not too happy about our relationship."

This time, when he tried to pull her closer, she let him. Resting her cheek on his chest, she pulled in a deep, unsteady breath.

If only she could close her eyes and all her troubles with Neil would just disappear. Colin was being so good about this. So supportive.

He deserved the same cooperation from her.

"Colin, I've been thinking about the DNA testing. I've decided it's something that has to be done."

"Really?"

The hope in his eyes made Sally feel guilty for not following up on this sooner.

"I'm still not sure what I'm going to tell Lara."

"Chances are Neil is her father and you won't have to tell her anything."

"But I need a sample of her saliva."

Colin rubbed his chin. "Well, you could rub the

cotton swab inside her cheek when she's sleeping. She wouldn't have to know."

Sally frowned. Something about that felt wrong to her. On the other hand, if Neil turned out to be the biological father, it would be a shame to have worried Lara over nothing.

"Pick up the kit," she told Collin. "And I'll do it."

"Thank you, Sally. This means so much to me." Colin's head dipped toward hers and their lips met. He put a hand behind her head and held her there. With each tender kiss, Sally could feel the life pulsing back into her limbs.

She was so tired of worrying about Neil. Of fretting about the consequences of her every action.

Colin fell back to the sofa, bringing her with him. *Oh, I want…I want…*

Her desires never made it to the top of her to-do list, but tonight the calendar was clear, and for the first time in a long, long while, she let her mind sink beneath the weight of her feelings.

His hands sliding down her back, under her shirt…

His lips, his mouth, the deepest kiss she could ever remember…

His body, long and hard, under hers.

Ah, Colin, Colin, Colin.

The pleasure of all this. How could she have lived so long without it? The loving touch of his hand on her breast, the building heat at her core, this driving, incredible need for skin against skin.

The sofa was too stifling, so they fell to the floor, Colin absorbing the shock with his body. Their jerseys slid off easily, the jeans were a nuisance, stiff zippers and rough denim.

At last she could feel him, all of him. Her hands and mouth explored as pleasure mounted to dizzying levels.

Colin caught her, held her still. "Sally, I've wanted you for so long."

She didn't ask how long. She knew.

Guilt stabbed her then. Oh, Beth. Beth. She closed her eyes against wet tears. Where had they come from?

Colin kissed her eyes softly. "It's okay, Sally."

Was this wrong? Sally couldn't say. All she knew was that she still wanted him. Memories of Beth, worries about Lara, fears of Neil, all of these were pushed to the side by the heavy, aching need that claimed her tonight.

"Make love to me, Colin."

He rose to his knees, grabbed for his jeans, for a condom in the pocket. She flashed back sixteen years, remembering him doing this before. Sheathing himself, then bending over her again. His warm words murmured into her ear might have been the very same words.

Her name, repeated over and over and over.

And then he was inside her, satisfying one hunger, only to create another.

Yes. More. More.

She wanted so much it scared her. Not just this, but him. Not just tonight, but forever.

Her feelings were definitely in control now.

"Sally."

She took one quick breath. Then shattered, her pleasure exploding in waves. She heard his cry and hers, blending into one.

Then silence. Exhausted, hopeful, tender silence.

Sally rested her head on his chest and heard the thumping of his heart in her ear. This was a good sound, one of the very best. Colin reached for a throw on a nearby chair and covered them both. She felt as if she could sleep here all night with one of his hands on her waist, the other tangled in her hair.

"Oh my love," he said, so softly she couldn't be sure of the words.

Ten minutes later he was asleep, they both were, or maybe she'd just been on the verge, because the noise of a car engine revving out on the street shouldn't have been enough to wake her up.

A car.

Neil.

No, it wasn't possible. This was his weekend with

Lara. He wouldn't leave their daughter alone in his condo in the middle of the night.

Sally closed her eyes and slept.

CHAPTER FIFTEEN

SALLY WAS GLAD to have the afternoon to herself before Lara came home. She wanted to savor the events of the previous night—every detail, every word, every look.

She was glad that Colin had left after their breakfast together. It had been simple but cozy: coffee, toast and the Sunday paper. A lovely way to spend a lazy weekend morning. She suspected Colin would have been happy to go back to bed after that, and part of her had wanted the same thing.

But she'd needed some reflection time, and Colin had been gracious about accepting that. Of all the things she loved about Colin—and there were many—she thought his ability to be flexible, to change his plans to fit in with hers, was what she appreciated most.

With Neil she'd been on edge all the time, trying to meet his expectations. What bliss to actually relax with her lover. To speak thoughts without censorship. To joke and laugh and…breathe!

That's why she felt so different this morning. She'd been in some sort of emotional prison and hadn't even realized it. Why had she let Neil do that to her? What had she been so afraid of?

A smashed car? A broken window?

It was pathetic, looking back, to see how she had backpedaled and accommodated and smoothed over so many of Neil's tantrums and all for the sake of what…keeping peace? Making Lara happy?

But Lara hadn't been fooled by any of that.

And now, thank goodness, neither was Sally. She felt happy and free and the only thing that put a damper on her day was thinking of Beth and wondering if it was right for her to be so happy when Beth could not be. Not now. Not ever.

The logical side of her brain knew this was ridiculous. Beth was gone. Denying herself and Colin happiness would never change that.

But logic only went so far. There was no avoiding the emotional baggage that went along with falling in love with your best friend's widower.

How was Colin dealing with this, she wondered. He'd seemed in high spirits when he'd left her this morning, but she had no doubt that he would eventually go through the same self-examination.

Around three in the afternoon Sally went out for groceries. She bought a roasting chicken and vegetables, then went home to cook. By the time Neil's

Jag pulled up in her driveway, the house was filled with the scents of homemade gravy and potatoes roasted with rosemary.

Neil stayed in the car, while Sally remained rooted to the front porch. She watched Lara lug her duffel bag out of the trunk, then go to the driver's side window to kiss her father goodbye.

"Did you have a good weekend?" Sally could pick up no clues from her daughter's calm expression. She was always like this—controlled and quiet—when in proximity to both her and Neil.

"It was fine." Lara gave her a hello kiss, then passed through the entry and headed straight for her room.

Sally waited for Neil to drive off, but he didn't. He was staring at her, his trademark ice-man smile in place.

She willed him to leave, but he did the opposite, getting out of the car, then leaning against the roof. All the while he continued to smile at her. It was an indulgent, condescending sort of smile, as if he knew something she didn't.

"Well, well, Sally. Got some this weekend, did you?"

She hated him. She really hated him. "Go to hell, Neil."

Though he continued to smile, she could see that she'd irked him. Neil hated it when women cursed. Especially at him.

"The sex didn't do much for your mood. Maybe you ought to try a different man next time. A *real* man."

She'd held her tongue a thousand different times with this man and those days were over. "Get off my property."

"Is that any way to speak to your daughter's father?"

"It is when you speak to me the way you just did. Go, Neil."

"Or else what, Sal? Are you going to call the police? What will you accuse me of? Dropping off my daughter after the weekend? I wonder what the sentence for that crime is these days."

He would stand here taunting her for hours if she let him. She pulled out the cell phone strapped to her waist. "Let's let the police decide what to charge you with, shall we?"

"Give it a rest, Sal. I'm on my way."

She stopped dialing, hoping he couldn't see how her fingers were shaking. "So go, then."

He sneered. "You think you're such a hotshot, don't you? Justice Stowe in waiting. Well, don't get too attached to the title. Something tells me that after this week you'll be the last person who can expect a phone call from our esteemed minister of justice."

He'd threatened her before, but the confident wink he gave her sent chills down Sally's neck.

"What are you talking about?"

"You'll see, Sal. You'll see."

And then, finally, he left.

ON MONDAY MORNING, Sally was walking down Sixth Street toward her office when she saw the morning *Sun* in a newspaper box on the corner. Her eye was caught by a picture of a familiar-looking man coming out of a familiar-looking house. The only problem was the man—Rick Moore—didn't belong to the house—which was hers.

The headline made her feel like she was trapped in a bad movie. "Judge Candidate Sleeps With Client's Ex."

Cursing like a sailor, Sally dropped the requisite coins into the slot, then pulled out the top copy.

Standing on the street corner, she began to read.

Sally Stowe, a Calgary lawyer specializing in family law, appears to be having an affair with the ex-husband of one of her clients—a definite no-no according to the rules of conduct set out by the Law Society of Alberta. Stowe, rumored to be one of several possible candidates likely to replace Justice Kendal on the Court of Queen's Bench, is divorced with a sixteen-year-old daughter.

There was a picture of Sally farther down on the page. A picture that Sally did not recognize. She was standing at her front door—the same door that Rick was seen sneaking out of—looking disheveled, unprofessional and almost foolishly happy. With a shock she realized the photograph had been taken the morning after her night with Colin.

Oh my Lord, how was this possible?

A neighbor claims he saw a strange vehicle parked outside Ms. Stowe's home on Saturday night. Apparently Rick Moore—the ex-husband of one of Ms. Stowe's clients—spent the night, then snuck out early Sunday morning.

Sally dropped her arms. She couldn't process this. She glanced around and wondered if it was her imagination that several passersby were giving her second looks. Had they read the article? Could they recognize her from that awful picture?

She folded the paper under her arm and hurried for the sanctuary of her office.

By NINE-THIRTY, two of Sally's clients had canceled their appointments for later that day and Gerald Thornton and Willa Kendal had both expressed a wish to speak to her later in the afternoon.

Sally's head was pounding. She'd read the article in full from the relative quiet of her desk and was still confused. What had Rick Moore been doing in her house? Who had taken those pictures? And how had they gotten into the hands of that *Sun* reporter?

It had to be a setup. And if it was, then Neil had to be behind it all.

But how had he pulled it off? Rick Moore didn't run in Neil's social circles. How had the two men met?

Sally recalled Pam's excitement over the check Rick had recently sent her. Had Rick received the money from Neil? Surely not.

And yet… And yet.

Maybe Neil had somehow gained access to her client information. He would have recognized Rick from the newspaper coverage of the trash incident. He wasn't above using another man's hostility to serve his own purposes. Maybe he had contacted Rick with a proposition that would help the both of them.

Sally knew her theory was far-fetched, but it was the only one she could come up with. Unfortunately she couldn't imagine anyone believing her.

Which left her very little wiggle room.

Sally rubbed her temples, anticipating a head-ache that hadn't yet arrived.

And then her phone rang. It was Pam Moore.

Pam. Oh, God, she hadn't even considered what she was going to tell Pam.

"I guess you saw the paper."

At first there was only a choked sob at the other end of the line. Sally felt like crying, too, but took a deep breath instead.

"You know it isn't true, Pam. Right?"

"I—I don't know what to believe. Those pictures…" More sobbing. Sally's head started to throb.

"I can't explain those. All I can tell you is that I'm not involved with Rick. I've never even run across him when I wasn't with you."

"But he was coming out of your house! Don't tell me there's another house out there just like yours. That dried-flower wreath you bought at the farmer's market in Longview last fall is in the picture."

Oh, yes, it had been her house. No question about that. The house that she always kept locked, with the security alarm activated, and a guard-dog-in-training on the alert.

"He must have broken in somehow." It was lame, and Sally knew it, but she didn't have anything else.

"What about your security system?"

Yes. What about her security system? Was it not working properly?

Another possibility: Neil had a key to her house and had found out the code to her security system. Could Lara…?

"Pam, I know it's asking a lot, but please believe me. Rick did not spend the night at my house. I haven't even seen him for over a month…"

But Pam wasn't listening. "That's why he finally paid me the money he owed me, isn't it? Because you wanted me out of the picture. Maybe you even gave him the money?"

"Of course not!"

Pam stopped crying. Her voice became hard and cold. "The worst thing is that I thought you were my friend. I could take being betrayed by my lawyer a hell of lot easier than being deceived by a friend."

Sally stopped trying to defend herself. Pam clearly wasn't in the mood to listen. Not that she could blame her. She didn't have much of a case to support her position.

Damn Neil to hell and back. He'd not only managed to hurt her this time, but Pam, too. And Lara. Sally could just imagine what the kids at school were going to put her through today. She had to phone the school and pull her out of classes.

"Pam, let me call you later. I'm sure—"

"No. I don't want to talk to you ever again. Even lawyers must have professional standards. You can be sure I'll be getting a new attorney—and filing a complaint."

Suddenly the full ramifications of this nightmare became crystal clear to Sally. There was going to be an investigation. She probably wouldn't be disbarred, but her reputation would suffer.

And as for the judicial appointment. Well, as Neil had promised, that was completely out of her reach now.

As Sally punched in the number for her daughter's school, she thought about Colin. Had he seen the paper yet? She ought to give him a call. But wait a minute. Why hadn't he contacted her? She sure could use a little moral support around now.

Unless he believed the story, too? In which case her life was totally screwed.

CHAPTER SIXTEEN

A NEWS CREW from A-Channel was waiting for Sally when she stepped off the elevator into the lobby of her firm's building. She was so focused on the need to pick up her daughter that she didn't even notice until a microphone was shoved in front of her face.

"Can you tell us the name of the man who left your house early Sunday morning?"

Her mind went blank as she took in the melee around her. People, cameras, a bright, hot light.

"Is it true your lover is the ex-husband of one of your clients?"

The urge to seize this opportunity to deny everything was strong. It took a lot of willpower for Sally to utter a terse "No comment."

She wouldn't do her case any good by ranting to the press. Though she knew she'd been set up, she had no proof. None at all. She'd just look like a liar if she tried to deny the story that was so effectively portrayed in those photographs.

She brushed past the gaggle of journalists and

headed for the door to the parkade. Thankfully she wasn't followed as she drove the usual route to Lara's school.

On the way she broke her rule about not using her cell phone while she was driving and put in calls to both Willa and Gerald.

She didn't know if she was relieved or not when neither one was in their office. She left the same message with each of them.

"I'm not sure what's going on, but the allegations in today's paper are totally untrue. I'll try to call you later once I've had a chance to talk to my daughter."

And speaking of talking to Lara…whatever was she going to say to her? Sally would have preferred the truth—but she couldn't tell her daughter that this was all a scheme of her father's to keep her from getting that judicial appointment. She had to come up with something else.

Sally had no sooner parked in the circular driveway of the school's main entrance, than Lara, looking harried and vulnerable, came dashing toward her.

Lara settled into the car, then slammed the door. "I'm so glad you're here. What's going on, Mom?"

She turned her trusting face to her mother, seeking reassurance and Sally felt like crying with relief. *She doesn't believe it. Not a word.*

"The truth is…well, I can't say for sure. It's

complicated. Were the kids at school giving you a hard time?"

"Not really. A few of the guys made some rude comments."

Sally didn't ask for specifics.

"But I just told everyone it wasn't true. It isn't, right?" A worry line creased Lara's forehead.

"Of course not."

"That was Pam Moore's husband in the picture, though. Coming out of our house."

Lara had met Rick once when she'd been baby-sitting the kids. "Yes. That was Rick all right. I have no idea how he could have gotten inside our house. Aside from the pet-sitter, only you and I have keys *and* the security code." Colin had Beth's old key, but he didn't know the password for her security system.

Lara started biting the inside of her cheek.

"What's wrong, hon?"

"Dad knows, too."

Sally felt a cold sweat break out over her body. "I've never given your father a key to our house."

"He made a copy of mine. He said it was a good idea for him to have a way into the house in case of emergencies. Like if you were away on a business trip or something and…" Lara shrugged, clearly unable to remember the particulars of the example her father had given her.

"I suppose you've given him the security code, too, then?"

Lara nodded. "Shouldn't I have?"

Sally's body turned from cold to hot. If Neil had access to her house, then that explained everything. Getting in touch with Rick would have been easy. He could have copied the e-mail list of her business contacts from her home computer.

She also kept a spare set of office keys in the desk.

No question now, how Neil had managed to pull this off. Lara, her bright daughter, was obviously thinking along the same lines.

"Dad wouldn't have…"

Sally knew that Lara was not able to convince herself that this stunt was totally beyond her father's capabilities.

"Even if he could," Lara eventually said, "why would he want to hurt you that way?"

Sally hated to hear the pain behind the question. Why did Neil never consider the ramifications on their daughter before he acted? "I don't know, hon."

But of course she did know. She understood Neil's motivations all too well. Neil wanted to prevent her judicial appointment from coming through. He'd been clear about that from the beginning. She should have known better than to discount his ability to get what he wanted.

"There may be another explanation for this mess," she said. "The important thing right now is that you know what they insinuated in the paper isn't true. Pam is not only my client, she's a friend. If her husband was Brad Pitt, himself, I would never even consider…"

"I believe you, Mom."

If she hadn't been driving, Sally would have given Lara a bear hug. As it was, she contented herself with a huge smile. Then she remembered that there was something else that Lara needed to be told.

"The reporter did get one detail right, hon. I have started seeing someone. Not Rick Moore. Someone else."

"Beth's husband?"

Sally wished she hadn't chosen to put it that way, but she nodded. "That's right."

Lara considered this in silence. She still hadn't spoken by the time they reached home. Sally pulled the car into the garage, then leaned over to touch Lara's arm. "Are you upset that I'm dating Colin?"

"Not really. He's a good guy."

"It's kind of weird that he was Beth's husband though, isn't it?"

Lara nodded, looking relieved that Sally had been the one to say the words.

"It bothers me, too," Sally admitted. "But I keep thinking that Beth would have wanted Colin and me to be happy. She was a very kindhearted person. And generous."

"Yeah."

Lara didn't sound totally convinced, and Sally didn't blame her. How could she persuade her daughter she was doing the right thing, when she didn't believe it herself?

Tired, Sally got out of the car and went inside. Predictably Lara headed for her room, and after a moment's consideration, Sally decided to give her some space before continuing their conversation. She went to her home office and checked her e-mail. She'd already canceled her few remaining appointments of the day, leaving her all afternoon to catch up on paperwork.

A minute after she'd sat down, her cell phone rang. It was Willa, demanding answers. A few minutes later, Gerald called back, too. Neither seemed impressed with the explanation she gave them. Especially when she hinted that her ex-husband might have orchestrated the stunt.

It was just as she'd feared all along. Neil's legal reputation was too upstanding. If Willa and Gerald—her friends and supporters—had trouble believing her story, what luck did she have with the rest of the legal world?

Funny to remember how confident she'd been just yesterday. She'd thought she'd finally taken the upper hand with her ex-husband. What a joke. She would never be free of Neil and his machinations until one or the other of them was dead.

There was her answer. All she had to do to solve her problems was kill Neil.

She massaged her temples wearily. *I'm turning as crazy as he is.*

The ringing of the doorbell was a welcome diversion. Sally went to open the door, even though she suspected she would find a solicitor of one sort or another. She and Lara weren't usually home at this time, so it wouldn't be one of their friends.

But it was. As she pulled open the heavy oak door, she was surprised to see Colin on the front porch. He looked terrible. At first he just stood there with such a sad, sad look in his eyes.

And she knew. He'd seen the article. He thought it was true.

Sally didn't have the energy to attempt to convince him otherwise. All day long she'd been beaten down by one person after another. If the man she'd thought she was falling in love with could believe the worst of her, then what did any of it matter? The story might just as well be true.

"I'm sorry, Colin. I can't do this right now." She started to close the door, but he put his hand on the frame and she had to pause.

"I called your office as soon as I heard about the

story in the *Sun*. Evelyn told me you'd be working from home this afternoon. Are you okay? I can't believe anyone could stoop so low. Even Neil."

"You think Neil was behind this?"

"Who else could it be?"

The relief was dizzying. "I thought maybe you believed the story."

"Are you kidding? That picture of you was taken Sunday morning when I left. You think I don't remember exactly what you looked like when I was driving away? You have no idea how much will-power I needed not to turn around and drag you back into the bedroom."

"Oh, Colin." She fell into his waiting arms, happy to be engulfed by his warmth, his solid presence. He kissed her then, and she was even happier to lose herself further. But—

"Lara's home. I took her out of school."

Colin smoothed the hair back from her forehead. "Okay. Thanks for the warning. I was just about to carry you off to your room."

That was what she wanted, too. More than anything. Inspiration struck. "Let's go to the mountains, Colin. Book a room at Baker's Creek and wait until this all blows over."

"Lara?"

"She can stay with her father." Only Sally didn't feel great about that anymore. She'd always assumed

Lara was safe with Neil. But if her daughter suspected Neil had something to do with the story in the paper, then maybe Lara hadn't been as protected from Neil's dark side as Sally had hoped.

"As tempting as it would be to run and hide, we can't do that." Colin spoke gently but firmly. "This story could destroy your professional reputation. We can't let Neil do that to you."

"Can you think of any way to stop him? Because I sure can't. Unless we pool our resources and hire a hit man."

Colin didn't smile. Maybe because he sensed that she was half-serious.

"Come on. Let's sit down and brainstorm. I'm sure between the two of us we can come up with a better solution than homicide."

She led Colin to her home office, closing the door so Lara wouldn't inadvertently hear something she shouldn't if she happened down the hall. Colin went to the window. In this room the view was blocked by a sturdy blue spruce tree. Sally went to the opposite wall and leaned her hand against the bookcase.

"I need to come up with a reasonable explanation for those pictures, a story that everyone will swallow."

Colin shook his head. "No. You need to prove the truth. That your ex-husband set you up."

"But I can't. That's the problem. Not unless Rick

decides to confess the truth…fat chance of that happening. I'm sure Neil paid him very well."

"But how did they get access to your house? That picture of Rick shows him actually stepping out of your front door."

She told him about the key and the password. "Neil's had them for years, according to Lara." The very idea creeped her out. She'd already changed the security code. Tomorrow she would phone for new locks.

"Any idea how Neil connected with Rick Moore?"

"I've been wondering about that, too. My best guess is that Neil remembered Rick from that article about him dumping trash in Pam's front yard. I suppose he found Rick's phone number in my electronic Day-Timer. Or he tracked him down some other way."

Colin shook his head with reluctant admiration. "He was smart to pick someone he knew would have a grudge against you. He must have paid Rick to pose for that photograph coming out of your door. Rick was probably only too glad to oblige, given that you were his ex's attorney."

"Rick has his own reasons to resent me," Sally agreed, wrapping her arms around her body. "I told you Neil was smart."

Colin must have sensed how beaten she felt, because he crossed the room and held out his arms again.

"Yeah, he's smart all right. The file of mine that went missing the other week? Well, it made a miraculous reappearance on the reception desk of our office this week. Now I can't even think about trying to nail him for theft."

"I'm sorry. You didn't have to worry about things like this before you became involved with me."

"Don't apologize. I told you we were in this together. Neil may be clever, but so are we. Let me call one of the investigators we use at work. Maybe we can catch Neil at his own game."

FROM THE COMFORT of his own home, Neil read the article on the front page of the *Sun* for about the tenth time that day. He couldn't stop smiling. If he'd written the damn piece himself, he couldn't be more pleased with the way it had turned out.

For the first time since his divorce from Sally, life was finally going his way. His ex-wife's career would never survive this. Oh, the alleged affair wasn't grounds for disbarment, but there would be an investigation and the bad press alone would be enough to kill her chances of becoming a judge. Not only that— her practice was sure to suffer as well. She'd never be viewed the same way by the legal profession as a whole.

Damn, but he was good.

He picked up the phone and called Rick.

"Did you see the paper?" was the first thing the other man asked him.

"I did. Good work, Moore."

"So the other half of the money…"

"Next Monday, like we agreed. I'll meet you at the same diner as last time. Twelve, noon."

"Why do I have to wait a week? You got what you were after, now I want mine."

"Yes, but we need to be careful. If anyone sees us together, everything will be ruined."

"Then let's meet at night when it's dark—"

"No way." Neil cut him off firmly. "We're sticking to the agreement."

He hung up, annoyed, and his annoyance grew when the phone ran almost immediately again. He picked up and growled into the receiver, "I told you—"

"Neil? Is that you?"

Neil's stomach dropped as he recognized his mother's voice. Each word enunciated with ball-splitting precision. "Hello, Mum."

"Why did you yell into the telephone?"

"I'm sorry. I thought you were someone else." He knew his mother would find that no excuse for such poor manners and continued quickly, "Are you calling for details about our summer travel plans?"

"Of course I am. I've been leaving you messages for weeks. Why haven't you returned my calls? For all you knew, I could have been laid up in hospital…"

She carried on in that vein for a while. When his mother was upset, she needed to vent.

Like after the first time she'd met Sally.

His mother had disapproved of Neil's choice of a bride. She blamed Sally single-handedly for keeping her son in North America, and she had been openly hostile to Sally during her one visit to Calgary, shortly after Lara was born.

When she'd heard about the divorce, she'd assured Neil that she'd seen it coming. Then she'd asked him how soon she could expect him home. He'd been glad there was an ocean between them when he told her he was staying.

Lara was his excuse, but in truth, he preferred living on a separate continent from his mother.

She'd always been a critical sort of person. But he knew she was going to love Lara. How could she not?

"I'm sorry, Mum. It's been a busy time."

"How can you be too busy to phone your mother? Now—" his mother's voice deepened, became even more autocratic "—have you booked your flights?"

"Everything's arranged." He opened the Day-Timer where he'd recorded the information. "Lara's passport came through last week. We'll be flying Air Canada." He gave her the flight numbers and arrival time.

"I'll send a car," his mother said. She asked several more questions about the trip and Neil answered each patiently and politely.

"Lara is very excited about meeting you, Mum." His mother had seen his daughter only that once, when Lara was a baby. Though he and Sally had had a guest room, his mother had refused to stay with them. Their home was too small, she'd said. Besides she preferred room service to home cooking. Her excuses hadn't fooled anyone, least of all Sally.

"Well, I'll be interested to see how she's turned out. She was a well-behaved baby, I'll give her that."

"She's turning into a wonderful young lady. She's in the top ten percent of her class and her skiing—"

"Yes, you've told me about all that." His mother sounded impatient. "I'm more interested in her manners and how she conducts herself."

Neil felt a momentary panic. He'd meant to enroll Lara in etiquette classes to prepare her for the trip. Lara's behavior certainly exceeded the average North American standards, but he knew his mother's were much higher.

He inquired about his aunt Jacqueline's health, and his mother's pet dog, Duster, then he rang off.

He made a note for himself about the etiquette lessons. Maybe he could book a private session for Lara. That would be best.

Neil grilled himself a lean steak and a tomato for supper. He always ate carefully, watching portion control in order to maintain his trim physique.

After his meal, he cleaned the kitchen, disinfecting both the sink and the counters. When he'd met Rick Moore in the diner last week, he'd been appalled at the other man's slovenly habits. He'd spoken with his mouth full, tried to smoke during the meal, until their server reminded him of the antismoking laws. And, most unbelievably, he'd actually combed his hair at the table, while they were waiting for the check.

His mother was right about one thing, Neil concluded. North Americans were pigs.

It wasn't until he was lying in bed ready for sleep that he started thinking about Sally and Colin again. Were they together right now?

He hated the idea of Sally being with Colin Foster, even more than he'd hated the idea of the other men she'd dated since their divorce. It didn't help remembering that the last time he'd squared off against Foster in the courtroom, Foster had come out the winner.

And now he was claiming Neil's wife, as well.

It has to stop.

But how? Neil had a feeling the tactics that had been successful in the past wouldn't work this time.

He needed something else. Something that would be one-hundred-percent effective.

CHAPTER SEVENTEEN

WHILE THE MAIN PURPOSE of Colin's visit had been to offer Sally moral support, he'd also left something with her. Later that night, about an hour after Lara had turned out her bedroom light, Sally crept down the hall with the cotton swab in one hand, a sterile container in the other.

Colin's unflinching trust and loyalty today had only strengthened her resolve to do this for him. To obtain a sample of her daughter's DNA so that he— and she—could finally know whether he was the biological father or not.

Sally paused by her daughter's door, then slowly opened it.

Bundled under her down duvet, Lara was soundly asleep.

Sally crossed to her daughter's bed. Lara was on her back, her head turned to one side, her mouth gaping slightly.

That one-inch space would make what Sally needed to do easy.

And yet, she couldn't seem to do it. Sally brought the cotton swab toward her daughter's face then moved it away.

Lord help her, this felt sneaky. And wrong.

But Colin deserved the truth. And Lara didn't need to know about the test if it proved what they'd always assumed…that Neil was her father.

So do it, Sally. Get the sample and leave.

Instead of swiping the cotton along the inside of her daughter's cheek, though, Sally perched on the side of Lara's bed and stroked the side of the sleeping girl's face.

Lara's eyes opened. "Mom? Is something wrong?"

Sally waited a few moments, until she was certain Lara was completely awake.

"You know how I told you that Colin and I are seeing each other now?"

"Yeah."

"Well, we went out once before. A long time ago. Before Colin was married to Beth and before I married your father."

Lara propped herself up on her elbows. Her eyes were large and wary as if she guessed she wasn't going to like this.

"The thing is, Lara, I slept with Colin about a week before I slept with your dad."

"Oh my God, Mom." Lara screwed up her face. "Why are you telling me this?"

"I wasn't promiscuous. Not usually. It's just that I didn't know Beth liked Colin and when I found out that she did, I wanted to forget about him as fast as I could. That's why I started up with your dad. He asked me out every night that first week and we ended up in bed on the fourth date."

Lara covered her face with her hands.

"I'm sorry. I know you'd have been happy without knowing all these details. But I had to tell you so you could understand something."

Lara spread her fingers so she could peek out at her mother. "What?"

Sally took a deep breath. "There's a possibility that Colin Foster could be your biological father."

"What?" Lara drew her knees to her chest and wrapped her arms around her legs, forming a tight, solitary ball. She frowned as she processed her mother's words, then shook her head. "No." Then louder. *"No."*

"It's just a remote possibility, hon." As if that made it any better.

Lara's features stiffened with distrust. "Why are you telling me this now? Were you and Dad fighting again?"

"Oh, hon. This isn't about your father and me. Colin was the one—" She stopped. It wasn't fair to lay the blame on Colin just because he'd been the first to ask the question. "I'm almost certain that Neil *is* your father."

"Then why are you telling me this?"

"Because I think we need to know the truth. Colin and I…and even you."

Lara said nothing to that. Sally tried to put a re-assuring hand on her back, but Lara winced and pulled away. *Oh, my baby. This is so unfair to you.* Maybe she should have taken the swab while Lara was sleeping. But too late now. Pandora's box was well and truly opened.

"I don't understand why this is coming up now."

"It's not easy to explain. I'd been seeing Neil for several months when I found out I was pregnant. I guess I didn't even want to consider the possibility that he wasn't the father. But I should have. I have no excuse there."

"So…Colin Foster really could be my dad?" Lara swallowed. "It's like…possible?"

"Yes."

"But—" Lara looked like she wanted to argue the point but couldn't. She glared at Sally, her face full of frustration. Then her gaze dropped to the cotton swab. "What's that?"

Sally explained about the DNA test and how it worked.

"So we get the results in a week?"

"That's right."

Lara's chest rose, then fell on a heavy sigh. Without making eye contact with her mother, she reached out her hand. After a brief pause, Sally passed her the swab.

Lara stared at it. "So I wipe the inside of my cheek with this?"

"That's right. Then it has to go straight into this bag—" Sally held it up for her to see "—so the sample isn't contaminated."

Lara hesitated for a long moment, then brought the stick to her mouth. When she was done, she dropped it into the bag, still not meeting her mother's eyes.

Sally wasn't sure what to say. "Thank you, Lara. I hope—" She stopped. What *did* she hope? That Neil was the real father? Or Colin? "I hope you know that whatever—"

Lara turned her head deliberately to the opposite wall. "You got what you wanted, Mom. Could you leave me alone now?"

Reluctantly, Sally stood. Lara's bottom lip was trembling. Her daughter was about to burst into tears. "This has been a terrible shock. If you want to talk—"

"I don't want to talk. Especially not to you. Just leave me alone."

The urge to reach out to her daughter was overpowering. And yet Sally didn't. She couldn't blame Lara for rejecting her. She'd just shattered the very foundation of Lara's life. As if the divorce hadn't been hard enough.

Slowly Sally made her way to the doorway. When she glanced back, Lara had squirreled under the covers.

"I love you, honey."

No reply. Not that Sally had expected one. But still, Lara's silence hurt. She glanced down at the plastic bag in her hand and wondered if the DNA code within would make matters better…or worse.

A WEEK AFTER the humiliating publication of Sally's supposed love affair with her client's ex-husband, she received an official-looking letter in the morning post at work. Evelyn placed the envelope in her hand with an apologetic shrug. They both knew what it contained.

Sally waited until she was alone to tear it open. As she'd expected, the law society was giving her notice that her client, Pamela Moore, had filed a conflict-of-interest complaint.

Sally had been warned that the article in the *Sun* would lead to an investigation. But seeing the evidence in black and white before her—the letter signed by a man she considered a friend as well as a respected colleague—was harder than she'd anticipated. As she refolded the letter, she felt tears forming behind her eyes.

She blinked, distracting herself from her predicament by trying to remember the last time she'd cried. It had been about a month after Beth's funeral. She'd had one of those automatic impulses to give her friend a call. Funny how that old habit had been so difficult to break. That time, she'd caught herself before actually dialing the number. But there had been a terrible poignancy to the moment, a true realization that she would never be able to call Beth again, and she'd burst into tears. Her crying jag had gone on for at least an hour.

But she couldn't allow herself to break down today. Certainly not here at the office.

Several days ago Gerald had suggested a few weeks' holiday might be in order. At the time she'd resisted, worried about giving the appearance of guilt. But concentrating on work was harder than she'd thought. And now that she had an official investigation to worry about, that was only going to get worse.

She stepped out into the hall and crossed to Gerald's office. He was on the phone, but he waved her inside. After a brief moment he concluded his call. She handed him the letter from the law society.

"Well," he said, after reading it. "We knew this was inevitable." As his eyes sought hers from above his half-moon glasses, she found herself avoiding the contact. Her gaze shifted around the familiar office, settling on a family photograph taken several Christmas seasons ago. She knew Gerald's wife well and was familiar with his university-aged sons, too.

The Thorntons invited her and Lara to their Christmas Eve celebrations every year. They were almost family.

"This is bloody hard, Sally."

She felt bad for Gerald and guessed that he was waiting for her apology. But she'd done nothing wrong. It disillusioned her that so few in her inner circle seemed ready to take that fact on faith.

"Maybe a few weeks away from the office wouldn't be such a bad idea," she said.

Gerald hesitated for almost a full minute. Then he sighed and handed her back the letter. "I think that's a wise decision. I'm sure the other partners will approve."

He said nothing more, but in his voice she heard the unspoken disappointment. Gerald had expected big things from her. This was the first time she'd let him down.

And what a letdown. A scandal of the front-page-news variety.

She bit back the urge to blurt out another plea of innocence. She'd already given him her version of the story. In their business, such pleas were a dime a dozen. Evidence was what counted. And in this case all of it was stacked against her.

She returned to her office and filled her briefcase with the few odds and ends that might need attending to in the upcoming weeks. There wasn't much.

She'd already reassigned most of her clients. She wondered if she would be able to reclaim them later.

But maybe the female clients wouldn't want to be reclaimed. After all, what woman would retain an attorney who might end up sleeping with the husband she was in the process of divorcing?

Sally arrived home several hours before Lara's school bus would show up. She poked around the garden for a while, then cooked a large batch of tomato sauce for dinner. While it was simmering, Lara called to remind her she had a driving lesson after school. Later, she was invited to a friend's house for dinner and to study.

"The driving instructor will drop me off at Jessica's. And since Jessica got her license last week, she can bring me home when we're finished working on our project."

Reluctantly, Sally gave her permission.

Lara hadn't been spending much time at home since the night she'd consented to give Sally the DNA sample. It was to be expected, Sally knew. Lara needed time to process. Yet she missed her daughter's company and the close bond they'd always shared.

Setting down the receiver and picking up the wooden spoon, Sally returned to the pot of simmering tomato sauce. She had way too much if Lara wasn't going to be home for dinner. She supposed she could freeze it.

As she was in the process of transferring ladle-fuls to plastic containers, her doorbell rang. Armani, who had been supervising her cooking efforts, on the alert for any spills, turned his attention to the front entry. His ears perked forward and he let out one sharp bark, before turning to her for further instruction.

At the door, Sally checked through the peephole, then gave the dog a reassuring pat. "It's a friend, Armani." She opened the door to Colin, who was still in his suit. He must have come straight from the office.

"Hi."

"Hi." His smile was intimate, as was his touch on her waist as he pulled her near for a kiss. "It smells good in here."

"I was cooking." Had her subconscious somehow hoped she could conjure Colin's appearance on her doorstep with a batch of his favorite food? If so, the ploy had worked and she was glad. They hadn't seen each other all week.

"I've missed you." He kissed her again, as if to show her how much.

"My life's been a little crazy." She found herself pulling back from his embrace. Not that she didn't want it, it was more that she felt…unworthy.

That was the source of the problem, she realized, the negativity she'd been feeling all week, and especially earlier in Gerald's office. She'd done nothing wrong, yet she felt tainted by the accusations made by that vile reporter. No wonder her clients wanted nothing to do with her. She felt the same way. And Colin, how did he feel? She examined his face carefully, searching for the smallest sign of distaste or discomfort.

"I hear you're officially on vacation." Colin's eyes told her that somehow he knew about the letter.

"Yes. Once I received notification that I was under investigation by the law society it seemed impossible to carry on as if nothing had changed. My partners had been trying to convince me to take a break for days. I'm sure they were very relieved by my decision."

"You know you'll be back. That in the long run your career won't be affected."

Did he really believe that? Sally wished that she could. "I should finish putting the sauce into the freezer. Mind watching me work?"

He followed her to the kitchen and tried to help her, but she kept spilling the sauce onto the counter.

"Sally." Colin gently removed the ladle from her hand. "This isn't over yet. You will be vindicated."

"You can't really believe that. My reputation has been shot. I'll never be able to prove those photographs were fakes."

"Yes, we will."

"How?" She looked at him. "Has that investigator you hired actually found anything helpful?"

"Not yet. But—"

Sally felt a frisson of anger. "Don't you see? Neil's too smart to make a mistake. He didn't want me to become a judge and now I most assuredly won't be. I'm not even sure I have a job any longer."

Suddenly she was assailed by the same weak urge to cry that she'd felt earlier. Ferociously she grabbed the ladle back and sloshed more sauce into the next container.

"Don't give up, Sally."

Colin wrapped his arms around her this time. She tried to resist, but eventually the anger seeped out of her.

The truth was, it felt wonderful to be comforted this way. She'd been alone for so many years and even when she had been married, Neil had been the source of her troubles, never a sanctuary.

"So few of my friends have been supportive, but you…" She couldn't complete the sentence. Couldn't put into words how much his trust meant to her.

She tipped her head back to study the depths of his eyes. And what she saw there made her remember, with a jolt, that more than a week had passed since she'd given him the saliva samples.

She pulled back a little, still keeping her hands on his shoulders, while his settled on her waist.

"You've heard back on the paternity test."

He nodded, his eyes gleaming.

She let her hands drop to her side, suddenly unable to breathe. Colin looked happy. But worried, too.

"You're Lara's father."

"I am."

CHAPTER EIGHTEEN

"Oʜ, Cᴏʟɪɴ." Suddenly Sally realized how much she'd hoped for the opposite result. So much of her life—and all of Lara's—had been predicated on the assumption that Neil was her baby's father.

If she'd known this sixteen years ago, would she even have married Neil? Would she have told Colin the truth? And, what about Beth?

"This is too much. I can't believe it. All these years…and I never guessed."

Colin stood back as she began to pace.

"I know it's overwhelming," he said. "I can hardly believe it myself."

Sally stopped in her tracks. "You must feel incredibly cheated."

"In one way, yes. But for years I've been resigned to the idea that I would never be a father. So, in another way I feel like I've just been handed the greatest gift of my life."

Sally put her hands to her mouth, afraid, yet again, that she was going to cry.

"I know Lara will be confused at first. Maybe even angry. I certainly don't expect her to stop loving Neil and thinking of him as her father. But maybe over time she'll come to feel some affection for me, too."

Sally couldn't believe how generous he was being. "It may take Lara a while to get used to the idea."

"That's okay. I'm in this for the long haul. And I'm talking about you, as well as Lara." He moved closer and placed his hands on either side of her face. "I'm in love with you, Sally."

Neil must have said those words to her once, but Sally felt as if she was hearing them for the first time in her life. And now she couldn't stop the tears that had threatened all day. They spilled from her eyes to the fine cotton of Colin's white shirt.

"Does that make you sad?" he whispered, sounding stricken.

She shook her head mutely.

"Then why are you—? Sally, talk to me. Tell me what you're thinking."

She inhaled deeply. Felt his fingers tenderly brushing the tears from her cheeks.

"It isn't fair to you, Colin. You've seen what Neil is capable of. If he finds out about this, he'll be furious. Lara means everything to him. Everything."

"I can deal with Neil. We can deal with him together."

How could he sound so confident? Especially when the worst still lay before them—telling Lara that Neil wasn't her biological father.

WHEN LARA FINALLY came home after studying with Jessica, Sally asked her to sit in the family room.

The TV was off. No music played on the stereo. The house was almost eerily silent.

Lara's back was rigid. She held her hands folded on her lap.

"Did the test results come back?" Her voice was cool and businesslike, but Sally could see that her daughter was holding back tears.

"Yes." She drew in a deep breath. "It turns out Colin was the father." *The* father. Not *your* father. It seemed safer to keep this impersonal for now.

Sally went to sit beside her daughter. "I'm so sorry, honey. I know this must be an awful shock." She put an arm around Lara's shoulders, but her daughter stiffened and pulled away.

Lara shimmied to the far end of the sofa. Her face reddened and her voice grew louder. "What's Dad going to say when he finds out? Wait—I guess I shouldn't call him that anymore, should I?"

"Of course you should! Neil is still your father. He raised you—he loves you."

"Yeah, *now* he does." Lara went suddenly quiet. Then, she whispered, "Do we have to tell him?"

Sally had been wondering the same thing. "Not right away we don't. This is a shock to me, too, hon. And to Colin. We all need a little time."

"Colin. Man, I'm going to feel so weird the next time I see him. I hope he doesn't expect me to call him Daddy now."

"Of course not. Nothing has to change between you and Colin. He knows you have a good relationship with your father and he doesn't want to jeopardize that."

"Then he shouldn't have made us take that stupid test!" Lara threw a cushion across the floor, then jumped off the sofa and began to pace. "This sucks, Mom. It really sucks."

What could she say to make this easier for Lara? "I'm sorry…" *Pathetic.*

"So what do I tell my friends?"

"I'd suggest nothing for now. At least, not until your father's been informed."

"So we *do* have to tell him?"

"Probably one day."

Lara shook her head. "This is so weird. You do realize that this is the sort of thing that happens on *Oprah.* Not in real life."

Sally laughed, but not without a touch of bitterness. It hurt to realize that her family had become perfect fodder for the talk-show circuit.

"I am so sorry, Lara. You're a great kid, growing

up to be a wonderful young woman. You didn't deserve a bombshell like this."

And neither did I.

ON TUESDAY, Sally dropped Lara off at school as
usual, then headed home. She still wasn't used to this
change in her routine and missed the half-hour commute to her office. Armani greeted her after being re-
leased from his exile in the laundry room, with an
excited wiggle and several licks of her hand.

At least he was happy that she no longer went to
work every day.

She took a mug of coffee to her home office, and
after watching Sally for several minutes, Armani
settled into the armchair in the corner of the room.
Sally opened yesterday's mail while she waited for
her computer to boot up.

There was only one message in her electronic in-
box this morning, from Willa.

Sally, I've been thinking about what you told me
and I honestly don't know what to believe. While
I can't fathom that you would be so foolish as to
get involved with your client's ex-husband, I like-
wise find it difficult to believe that Neil set you up
in such a diabolical manner.

God, Neil was so manipulative. He'd purposefully set out to charm Willa—and he sure succeeded. Sally wanted to scream. She read on.

Willa's message concluded with a final, cutting blow.

While I continue to hold you in high regard and wish the best for your future, in light of this recent scandal, I'm sure you will understand that I will no longer be able to recommend you for a position on the Queen's Bench.

Damn Neil! Damn him. She couldn't let him get away with this. There had to be *something* she could do.

Colin had pinned his hopes on the investigator he'd hired, but Sally felt the need to do more. Would Rick Moore crumble if she questioned him personally? Surely it was worth a try.

"I LOVE YOU, Daddy."

"I love you, too, sport." Neil hung up the phone thoughtfully. What was going on with Lara? She didn't usually call him at work, unless it was to ask him for something. A ride to a friend's house, a new set of skis, an increase in her allowance.

This call had been about nothing. Except that strange, hypothetical question. *Dad, if you found out*

*I wasn't your real kid—say you and Mom brought
the wrong baby home from the hospital—would you
still love me?*

When she was younger, Lara had posed all sorts
of weird questions. When she was eight, for instance,
he remembered her asking if he'd ever wished she
were a boy.

But she was sixteen now…so where was this sudden insecurity coming from?

Neil got up from behind his desk and went to the
window. Looking out over the office towers of
downtown Calgary, he wondered what Sally was
doing now that she was no longer working. On Saturday Lara had told him that her mother had been
encouraged to take some vacation time.

There'd been an accusatory note in his daughter's voice when she'd said that and it had been a
struggle for him to pretend to be sorry to hear the
news.

But of course, he'd already known. On Friday,
after "accidentally" bumping into Judge Kendal after
court and buying her a couple glasses of wine at
Marietta's, Neil had been privy to the whole scenario.

Pam Moore had filed an official complaint with
the law society and Sally was persona non grata at
Crane, Whyte and Thornton. On top of all that,

Willa Kendal confirmed that she was not going to be able to support Sally's bid for the Queen's Bench, after all.

It was all happening exactly as he'd planned. Sally's career was derailed, her life was a mess. He ought to be happy.

But suddenly destroying her career aspirations was no longer enough. Not now that she was seeing Colin Foster.

That was another tidbit Lara had dropped this weekend. They'd been throwing a football around at Bowness Park when she'd asked if he knew her mom was dating again.

He'd admitted that he did. Then he'd shut up, hoping she would keep talking. And she had.

She'd told him how weird she found it that her mom was going out with Auntie Beth's husband. Then she'd asked if he'd known that her mom had been involved with Colin years ago.

He'd almost stopped breathing. "How many years, sport?"

"Right before you two started dating. And I mean *right before*. Like days."

No, he hadn't known that. And now he wondered why Sally had never told him. And he wondered something else, too.

No. Every fiber in Neil's body resisted the idea. Lara was *his*. She meant everything to him.

And yet, hadn't he always wondered why she looked nothing like his side of the family? And what about her prowess at sports? That had never been his forte, but he knew Foster had almost made it to the Olympic ski team as a teenager.

Mixed in with his anger, Neil felt a kind of pain he'd never felt before. It reminded him of how he'd suffered when he'd realized Sally meant to divorce him.

Only this was worse. Much, much worse.

Neil went back to his desk and tossed back a couple of pain relievers from a bottle he kept in the top drawer. He planted his hands on the desk and allowed his head to droop. He could feel the blood pounding in and out of his skull and with each surge, his breath seemed to grow shorter.

He needed to get out of here. He grabbed his jacket, then dashed out to the hall, past the confused receptionist, who tried to ask him when she could expect him back. He was on an elevator before she could complete her sentence.

With screeching tires, he raced out of the underground parkade and by the time he'd hit the freeway and had worked up a little speed, he knew exactly what he had to do.

Lara was still at school, so Sally would be home alone. But before he tackled her, he needed to pick up something from his house. He had a few mementos from his meetings with Rick Moore that would cover his tracks perfectly.

CHAPTER NINETEEN

AFTER HER UNREWARDING meeting with Rick Moore—he'd refused to talk to her—Sally took Armani for a long walk along the river, revisiting paths she'd once frequented with Beth.

Armani was thrilled to be out in the fresh air, and the exercise and sunshine were soothing to Sally's state of mind. As she rounded a corner and came upon a wooden bench, her memory jolted her to the past. So often she and Beth had sat in this very spot, chatting intensely about whatever subject had caught their interest that day.

How she missed those talks with her best friend.

Sally sank onto the bench and looked out over the familiar view. The pale blue sky, streaked with white clouds, the winding river, the willows and tall grasses growing alongside of it.

Less than two months ago, her life had been right on track. Now her career was a mess, along with her professional reputation, and much worse, her relationship with her daughter was in jeopardy, too.

Given all that, what were the chances her relationship with Colin would be a success? It was bad enough that he'd been her best friend's husband. Now they had all the issues with Lara—and Neil, she couldn't ever forget Neil—to deal with as well.

Of all the problems, Neil was the one that frightened her most. She'd thought she could handle him. Now she knew she couldn't. Worse, what if he was to hurt Colin? Or Lara?

Sally closed her eyes and lifted her face toward the sun. *What should I do, Beth?*

But even if she were alive, her friend would probably have been unable to help. Sally had always shielded Beth from Neil's scarier side.

Sally thought about that night with Colin so many years ago. She and Colin had argued before. What had been so different that day? Why had she agreed to go to his place, where she'd ended up making love with him all night?

The next morning, when she'd hurried home to shower and change for her first class, she'd found Beth at the kitchen table, moaning over the new guy she'd been dating.

"He didn't call again last night. It's been a week, Sally. Do you think he isn't interested?"

Sally had been waiting for Beth to ask where she'd been. It wasn't as if she made a habit of spending the night out. But Beth had been totally preoccupied.

"Maybe you could try talking to him," Beth pleaded. "He's in his final year of law, just like you. Colin Foster. Do you know him?"

Colin Foster. Do you know him?

Those two sentences had changed everything. Stricken, Sally had ignored Colin that day, and when Neil Anderson had struck up a conversation with her, as he'd done before, this time she'd agreed to have lunch with him.

Colin had glowered at her throughout their class on civil procedure, but she'd sat with Neil and ignored Colin's increasingly desperate overtures. On the way out of class he'd pulled her aside.

"What the hell is going on here? Last night I thought—"

"Last night was a mistake. I'm going out with Neil tonight." She and Neil had dated exclusively after that.

Later, Beth had commented on the serendipity of the two of them falling in love within days of each other. After he'd given up on Sally, Colin had eventually called Beth. By then Sally and Neil were a steady item.

Sally had been so determined to keep her hands off her best friend's guy that she'd *made* herself fall in love with Neil. Or at least she'd convinced herself that was what had happened.

If she hadn't become pregnant, if she'd dated Neil

a little longer, she might have seen the warning signs. But everything happened so quickly. Beth and Colin were engaged right after graduation. It seemed only natural for her and Neil to follow in their footsteps.

Especially since Sally was pregnant.

Sally closed her eyes. Thinking of the past had made her weary. She felt a tug on the leash. Armani was bored of this rest stop. With a sigh, she pulled herself upright and headed for home.

AN HOUR LATER, Neil had control of his emotions again. He also had every last detail of his plan worked out.

Fortunately, his methodical nature was holding him in good stead. At home he'd found the comb Rick had left behind at the diner. He'd removed several strands of brown hair and placed them in what was now a sealed plastic bag, along with the button that had dropped off Rick's cuff during their lunch and the half-smoked cigarette that Neil had pocketed, after Rick ground it into the sidewalk.

That ought to be enough evidence, he figured.

Neil drove the Toyota again, parking it well down the block from Sally's house, then trotted quickly to the entrance at the back. She'd been out for a walk. He saw her sneakers, caked with mud, sitting on the back deck. The damn dog's leash was there, too, along with a plastic bag containing something vile that Neil didn't want to even think about.

Through the screen of an open window, he could hear music and the sound of Sally singing along. He noticed that she'd repaired the small square of glass he'd broken. The open window was above that—well out of his reach without a ladder.

From the cover of a lilac bush in full blossom, he crouched in front of the mullioned panes and cupped his hands over the glass so he could see inside. Sally was pulling ingredients from a cupboard.

It was too late for lunch, too early for dinner.

"Don't tell me she's finally learning to bake," he muttered under his breath. As she turned in his direction, he sank low, out of sight.

For several moments he waited. Then, when he heard the motor of a mixing machine start up in the kitchen, he tested the patio door.

Locked.

Undeterred, he pulled the key from his pocket. The damn thing wouldn't turn. He tried again, and again, before accepting that she must have changed the locks.

He hadn't counted on this. He crept back to the thick shrubs that bordered the deck and thought.

He could always break in. But a broken window wouldn't fit with the scenario he'd planned. He needed to come up with another idea. And soon. Lara's bus would be coming in about two hours and he wanted everything taken care of well before she arrived home.

Lara. Just thinking about his daughter was so incredibly painful. Did she have any idea that he might not be her real dad? He couldn't stand thinking about that.

The mixer inside the house turned off and in the sudden quiet, Neil could hear the chattering of a couple of squirrels in the spruce tree about twenty feet behind him. Reaching into his jacket, he found one of the protein bars he liked to keep on hand for Lara. He ripped the corner of the wrapper, then broke the bar into several pieces and tossed them into the shrubs next to the squirrels.

The rodents paused, then moved closer to investigate. A few seconds later, they were warring over the unexpected treats and making more noise than ever.

Neil glanced back into the kitchen. Sure enough the dog had raised his head at the sound of the squirrels. He sprang up and raced out of Neil's sight—presumably for the door. A moment later Sally let him outside and the dog shot from the house to the shrubs, barking like mad at the arguing rodents.

Neil listened carefully to the sound of the door closing. Had Sally reengaged the lock? He didn't think so.

Slowly, he crept out from his hiding spot. Fortunately the pup was so focused on the squirrels, he didn't notice Neil as he made his way toward the door.

His hand was damp with sweat when he gripped the knob. Gently he twisted it. There was a catch in the mechanism; the door inched forward.

It was open! He was in!

Neil wiped the knob with a cloth from his pocket, then pulled on a pair of latex gloves.

SALLY COULDN'T REMEMBER the last time she'd baked a cake. She wondered if it really mattered if you sifted the dry ingredients separately, then added them to the beaten butter, sugar, milk and eggs. Why dirty a second bowl when they were all going to end up together anyway?

She read the directions again, which definitely specified that the flour, salt and leavening agents should be combined in *a separate bowl.* Maybe she'd better do it their way. She didn't want to go to all this effort and have the cake not work out. With a sigh, she reached for a second bowl from the cupboard.

As she stood up, she caught a movement from the back door. She was surprised to see it wasn't fully closed. Hadn't she locked it after she let the dog out?

"Armani?" she called, knowing the dog wouldn't respond. She could hear him still barking at the squirrels in the backyard.

She started to move toward the door, then stopped at a suspicious sound. God, it sounded like somebody *breathing*...

Fear cut through her. No. It wasn't possible. She clasped her hands, her attention locked on the partially open door. Was it possible that Neil...?

And just as she thought his name, he was suddenly there, springing up from behind the kitchen island. She screamed as he reached out to grasp her hands. Twisting her body, he pulled her next to him, one hand covering her mouth.

His skin next to her mouth felt strangely smooth and smelled...different. She lowered her eyes and saw the latex gloves.

Why was he wearing gloves?

Her fear turned to terror.

AFTER A DAY SPENT in court, Colin was reviewing his voice-mail messages, while offhandedly sorting through the new files on his desk. His hands stilled at the sound of Harry Reiswig's deep baritone.

"Yeah, Colin, it's me, Harry. Just wanted to pass on an update on that job I've been handling for you. Give me a call on my cell."

Colin punched the number into his phone, even as the man was reciting it on the recording, then waited for the investigator to pick up.

Colin was almost afraid to hear what the man had

to say. He knew how devastated Sally would be if he failed, yet again, to turn up any evidence against her ex-husband.

The call was answered on the fifth ring. "Reiswig Investigations."

"Hey, Harry. This is Colin. You find anything?"

"Just a minute."

Colin could hear the sound of shuffling paper on the other end of the line. He shifted in his chair impatiently.

"Here it is," Harry said, finally. "That guy, that Neil Anderson…"

"Yes…?"

"He met someone at Bernie's Deli on Sixteenth Avenue yesterday afternoon."

Colin tempered his rising hope. "Who was it?"

"It was our guy. A definite match to that newspaper photo you showed me."

Well, hallelujah. This was exactly what they'd hoped for…to establish a connection between Rick Moore and Neil Anderson.

"Did you get the meeting on film, Harry?"

"You bet. And there's more good news. While I had the camera trained on them, an envelope was exchanged."

"From Anderson to Moore?" Colin couldn't stop the excitement from sounding in his voice.

"It happened just the way you guessed it would.

First the lawyer guy shows up, then the younger fellow. They order drinks and burgers and, after about fifteen minutes, the older guys passes the younger guy an envelope. The younger guy pockets the envelope then gets up to leave. Doesn't take more than a couple bites of the burger."

"Holy crap."

"Yup. I got the whole thing on video. Some digital photos, too."

Wait until he told Sally. Just wait until he told Sally! "Can you meet me in fifteen minutes?" he asked Harry. He wanted the evidence in hand when he broke the good news.

SALLY HAD NEVER CONSIDERED Neil an inherently violent man. Verbal swordplay was his specialty, subtle cruelty and mind games his preferred outlets for aggression.

But as he held her in a steellike grip with one arm, while reaching for her knife block with the other, she realized that the boundaries that had once held her ex-husband in check were now nonexistent.

"Neil," she tried to gasp, through the constraint of his hand over her mouth.

"You want to talk?" His fingers closed over one of the knives in the maple holder. Sally shut her eyes as he brought the cold steel to her throat. "That's good, Sal, because I want to listen."

Slowly he removed his hand from her mouth. She ran her tongue over her front teeth, tasting the metallic tang of fear.

With subtle pressure he reminded her of the presence of the knife at her throat. "Why don't you start by telling me who Lara's real father is? Is it Colin Foster?"

Lord help her. How could he have known to ask that? She couldn't let him guess the truth. She did her best to feign indignant anger. "Damn it, Neil. Have you gone crazy? What a stupid question. Put the knife away, for God's sake."

He pulled her body hard against his. She felt the press of his chest, his hips, his thighs. The pressure of the knife at her throat remained constant.

"Don't tell me what to do. Just answer the bloody question. Who is Lara's father?"

"Neil, this is insane." Her neck was beginning to ache from being held at this unusual angle. She didn't dare straighten it, however, not with the blade almost cutting into her flesh as it was.

"Answer the question, Sal. Just answer the bloody question!"

"*You* are Lara's father." Sally had no problem uttering the words with conviction. Lara *was* Neil's daughter in the truest sense of the word. "How can you doubt—" She gasped as he pulled his arm tighter across her stomach.

"I know that you slept with Colin when we were in law school."

How had he figured that out? She twisted slightly, as much as the knife would allow, and met his hard, bitter eyes. His lips stretched out in the ice-man smile.

"Don't you think should have told me, Sal? You slept with Colin Foster before you started going out with me. Maybe even after. He's the real reason you wanted a divorce, isn't he? You lying little slut…"

"Please, Neil. Let go of me. We need to talk."

"We're done talking. I can't have you in my life anymore."

His voice terrified her, almost as much as his words. His anger seemed spent now, replaced by a cold, fierce, determination. "Don't be stupid, Neil. They'll find you. The police will arrest you."

"Wrong again, Sal. The police will find *Rick Moore*. They'll arrest *him*."

"But—"

"Everything's all planned. I have samples of Rick's hair, a button from one of his shirts—even one of his disgusting half-smoked cigarettes. You want to know the way the story will play out? You tried to break off the relationship, but Rick wasn't willing. A lover's quarrel erupts, with the sad consequence of your death."

Oh, God, she should have known he would have

come here with a plan. Her mind raced with options. She could try to scratch him to get his skin cells under her fingernails.

But he would only scrape her nails clean after he'd killed her. Any residual traces of Neil in her house would be explained by his routine visits to pick up his daughter.

"What if Rick has an alibi for this afternoon?"

"He won't. I sent him on a little fool's errand that will make sure of that."

Sally's knees quivered. He'd considered every angle. Again, typical Neil.

"You're going to die, Sally."

It was true, she realized. She *was* going to die. Neil was going to win, like always.

"And once you're gone, Lara will be mine. All mine. She'll never know I'm not her father. And there'll be no living person who can tell her otherwise."

Lara already knew, but Sally was hardly going to tell Neil that. It wouldn't change anything, anyway. He was determined to kill her.

At the reminder of her daughter, though, Sally knew she couldn't let Neil win this time. Couldn't leave him alone with Lara, without her protection. To hell with the knife. She lashed out her arms, fighting with all her strength to wrench herself free.

Neil cursed as he fought to control her. "You

bloody bitch, what the hell do you think you're doing?"

Neil's voice had been steadily rising. Now he was shouting, and she could feel a sharp new pain at her throat. Had he cut through her skin?

"Neil! No!"

He covered her screams with his hand, but it was too late. The sound had carried through the open door and suddenly something was pushing that door open, running across the tiles, growling…

Armani. It was Armani. He leaped up to his hind feet and with his sharp teeth and strong jaw, took a firm grip on Neil's arm.

CHAPTER TWENTY

NEIL HOWLED with pain as the dog sank teeth through fabric into flesh. Sally heard the knife clatter on the floor at the same time as Neil's hold on her went slack. She scrambled along the floor toward Armani, who had let go of Neil's arm but was still growling.

"Get that animal away from me." Neil clenched his wounded arm, which was bleeding profusely.

Sally ignored him, putting a hand to Armani's back and using the counter to support her weight as she pulled herself erect. She grabbed the cell phone clipped to her waist and dialed 911.

"Get me some towels," Neil shouted at her. "He must have cut an artery. I'm bleeding to death here." He tried to stand up himself, but froze when Armani growled and made a move toward him.

Sally had never hated her ex-husband more, but she didn't want him torn to pieces. His wounded arm was bad enough. She put a hand on Armani's collar and held him tight. "That's a good boy, Armani. What a good boy."

"Towels?" Neil demanded again.

His face was deathly white and the blood continued to spurt from his arm. So maybe Armani *had* hit an artery. Sally put the phone down for a second in order to grab a few towels from the nearby drawer. She tossed them at Neil.

"Apply pressure to the wound," she told him, making sure to keep the dog between them, as she picked up the phone again.

Neil only managed a groan in response and then the 911 dispatcher came on the line. Sally recited her name and address.

"What seems to be the problem, ma'am?"

"My ex-husband just broke into my house and tried to kill me." She spoke the words calmly, but her heart was still racing and her hands shook so badly she could hardly hold the phone steady to her ear. "My dog attacked him and bit his arm. He's bleeding a lot."

Her eyes locked with Neil's. His eyes seemed out of focus. He was probably in shock. As her entire body began to shake, she realized she was, too.

"I'm not injured," she said in response to the dispatcher's next question, then remembering the pain she'd felt earlier, she put a hand to her throat. The blood had already clotted.

"Is he still armed?" the dispatcher asked.

"No." Sally eyed the knife, still lying on the floor where Neil had dropped it when Armani attacked. If he lunged, he could still reach it. But his eyes were closed. He must have passed out.

"He's lost a lot of blood," she told the dispatcher. "I think he's unconscious." Just to be sure, though, she ought to move that knife.

Sally tied Armani's leash to a supporting leg of the island—the dog was still growling and she didn't trust him not to go after Neil again, conscious or not. Then she reached for the knife.

She almost had it. But at the last moment, Neil's hand snaked out and grasped the weapon. She screamed and dropped the phone as he grabbed at her with surprising strength.

"Stop it, Neil! You'll aggravate the bleeding."

"I don't care if I bleed to death, as long as I take you with me."

Armani let loose with a frenzy of barking, as he pulled on his leash. Why had she been so foolish to tie him up? She should have let the dog chew Neil to pieces!

She felt the knife press against her throat again. Neil's blood—warm and sticky—soaked through her back and down her arm.

"You are going to pay, you bitch."

This time, Sally saw no room for hope. The emergency crew would take at least fifteen minutes to get here. In that amount of time…

She screamed again, praying a neighbor might

hear and come to her aid. Neil tried to cover her mouth with his hand, but in so doing, he loosened his hold on her waist and she wrenched herself free.

At just that moment, the back door swung fully open.

Colin burst into the room with a shout of fury. After an assessment of the scene that seemed to take less than a second, he lunged for Neil.

"He has a knife!" Sally saw Neil raise the blade toward Colin's face. As the two men struggled, she leaped at Neil's back, her hand grabbing for his raised wrist.

Together, she and Colin brought him to the kitchen floor. Neil swore and thrashed his arms and legs, as Colin twisted the knife from his grasp. With one swift maneuver, Colin had him on his stomach. Colin settled his weight on Neil's back, effectively immobilizing him.

Sally became aware of the distant whine of sirens. When Colin looked at her questioningly, she nodded. "I called 911 about five minutes ago." She glanced at the phone on the floor. "I never ended the connection. They're probably still on the line."

"Talk to them," Colin said between huffs of air.

She picked up the phone and tried to speak. Her voice failed her and she had to try again. Enunciating slowly out of necessity, she filled in the dispatcher with the latest events. She was instructed to stay on the line until help arrived, which, from the sound of the sirens, would be very soon.

Exhausted, Sally sank to the floor, still clasping the phone to her ear. Just ten feet away she could see Colin buck as Neil tried one last time to free himself. Finally Neil went limp. With his face pressed to the tile floor, he cursed.

"You son of a bitch," he said to Colin. "You slept with my wife."

"She isn't your wife anymore." Colin's voice was controlled, but the muscles in his shoulder and chest bunched visibly beneath his shirt from the effort of keeping Neil contained.

"You think I'm talking about the other week? I'm referring to Lara, you bastard. You slept with my wife before we were married. You're the one who fathered her child."

He let loose with more cursing, using words Sally had never heard him utter before.

"Shut up, you idiot." Colin jerked Neil's unwounded arm and pressed it hard against Neil's back. "Sally doesn't belong to you. Don't call her your wife ever again."

"Wh-what about Lara?" Neil's false bravado vanished. He glanced from Sally to Colin, the desperation naked in his eyes.

After a brief hesitation, Colin said, "Lara is your daughter."

Both men turned to Sally and she nodded her agreement. Neil did not deserve this generosity on Colin's part. But Lara did. And much as Lara might have conflicted feelings about Neil, she did love him. Sally would wait until her daughter was ready before she told Neil the truth.

AT SALLY'S REQUEST, Colin waited at the end of the block for Lara's school bus. He approached her as soon as she stepped off. Her initial smile was quickly replaced with a frown.

"What are you doing here, Mr. Foster?" She glanced in the direction of her house, her expression registering alarm at the sight of two police cars parked in the driveway.

Thankfully, the ambulance carrying her injured father had already left for the hospital.

Colin placed a hand gently on Lara's shoulder. "Your mother's fine, and your father will be, too. But there's been an incident…"

Lara's face turned white. "Daddy tried to kill her."

Amazing, Colin thought. The kid knew. But then, didn't kids always understand what was going on much better than their parents ever suspected?

"Your mom's fine," he repeated. "But Armani bit your dad's arm and he's lost a lot of blood. He'll probably be okay but they've taken him to the hospital."

"To the hospital?" Lara repeated, obviously in shock.

"Yes. Your mother wants you to come home with me for a while now. She'll meet us later."

Once she'd finished talking to the police. Sally had wanted to spare her daughter that much, as well as the sight of her father's blood streaked all over the kitchen floor.

"Will my dad go to jail?" Lara's eyes were wide and trusting as she trained them on Colin, waiting for his response.

And who better to give her one, Colin thought ironically, than a provincial crown prosecutor.

"Probably," he said, pulling no punches.

Lara swallowed, then nodded. "Okay."

He put his arm across her shoulders and began to lead her toward his car. She took a few steps, then jerked to a stop.

"Daddy!" she cried, throwing her hands in front of her face as she began to sob violently.

Colin had never held a child before, but he pulled Lara close as if he'd been doing it all his life.

"Your father will be okay," he murmured, hoping it was true. Hoping that Neil would learn from this experience. If anything could get the other man through the tough years ahead of him, surely it would be his love for the young woman Colin was now trying to console.

THE NEXT DAY Colin made an appointment with the officer in charge of the case and handed over Harry Reiswig's photographs. Rick Moore was hauled in for questioning and the next day the headline in the *Calgary Sun* screamed: Judicial Contender Framed By Ex-Husband. Alleged Affair A Scam.

Sally's final confrontation with Neil was also reported by the press. Sally did her best to downplay the incident, but the reporters loved the fact that her dog had come to her rescue. They were also thrilled to showcase a situation where an abused woman emerged from a confrontation with her violent ex-husband, victorious instead of dead.

That was how Sally was viewed now, despite years of trying to avoid the label in her own mind. An abused woman. An abused woman who had fought back...and won.

When Rick broke down and confessed his involvement in the scam to the police, Pam withdrew her complaint with the law society and called Sally to apologize.

Sally received a beautiful bouquet from the partners at Crane, Whyte and Thornton, as well as personal assurances from Gerald that regardless of the outcome of the judicial appointment, she would be welcome at the firm whenever she chose to come back.

Willa didn't call or send flowers. She visited Sally

on a warm Saturday morning and spoke to her with genuine humility. "Neil fooled many people and I'm sorry to say that I was one of them. Please forgive me, Sally. I should have placed more trust in your judgment than I did."

That night Lara went out with friends to a movie and Colin took Sally to Bragg Creek for dinner, then back to his place for coffee. They ended up, as usual, in his study. On the table in front of the sofa was a letter with Colin's name in Beth's handwriting.

Sally couldn't stop staring at the envelope and Colin didn't make her wait long.

"I finally cleared out Beth's closet. Sent most of the stuff to Goodwill. But guess what else I found? I've been waiting for a calm moment to show it to you."

He handed her the letter.

From the well-worn condition of the paper, Sally could tell that Colin had already read this numerous times. With her stomach wrung tight, like a water-logged towel, Sally unfolded the pages.

Dear Colin,
    These past few days I've been so tired. I know my time is running out. And so I must tell you something…something I wish I was strong enough to say in person.
    But I'm not that strong. And I console my-

self with the thought that now may not be the best time for you to hear this, either.

So I'm writing it all down and planning to tuck this letter away in my closet. I'm guessing you won't come across it until many months after I am gone. By then you will have found the birthday gift I left you in my car (I hope you liked it!) and the photographs I keep in my nightstand. Did you pause over the one of you and Sally? I'll bet you did. It was always a favorite of mine, too.

Sally stopped reading and glanced over at Colin. He stood by the window, his hands behind him on the ledge, his attention on her, expression solemn.

Where was Beth going with this? Colin's tense body language led her to expect the worst.

I do want you to find happiness once more after I am gone. If you are wondering if this means I give you my permission (not that you need it) to marry again, then you are right.

I even have an idea of whom you will marry. Don't be alarmed that I know this. You were the best husband that I could have hoped for and I never doubted that you loved me.

But I also realize that my happiness came with a cost paid by someone else. Sixteen years

*ago my best friend made a sacrifice on my be-
half and I let her do it. I didn't even admit that
I knew what she was giving up for me.*

So Beth had known who Sally was with that
night. And she'd never let on.

*I prayed that the choices she made as a
consequence would work out for her in the
end. But they didn't. Her marriage turned out
to be a dreadful mistake. And I know that is
partly my fault.*

No wonder Beth seemed so upset whenever Sally
tried to tell her about her problems with Neil.

*But there is another secret, Colin. Lara,
Sally's daughter, Lara, is your daughter, too.
I guessed this years ago, but I don't believe the
possibility has even occurred to Sally.*

*I'm sorry I never admitted that it was my
fault we couldn't have children. I'm sorry I
hurt my best friend and I'm sorry if I hurt you,
as well.*

*But would I change anything? Sometimes I
do ask myself that question. And I wish the answer could be different.*

I love you, Colin. So much, that if I were in

the same situation again, I would behave in exactly the same way. Please forgive me. Please be happy.

All my love,
Your faithful wife,
Beth

CHAPTER TWENTY-ONE

COLIN WATCHED as Sally refolded the letter and returned the pages to the envelope. He couldn't gauge her reaction, but he guessed she felt as shell-shocked as he had when he'd first read that letter.

He went to sit beside her. Took her cold hands between his warmer ones.

What was she thinking? She hadn't spoken since reading the letter. "Sally?"

Her gaze skimmed his, then settled on the envelope. She shook her head, as if still unable to believe what she'd just learned. "I always wondered if Beth knew it was you that I was with that night."

"I guess she did."

"How did she find out? I'm sure I never mentioned your name."

"Who knows? Maybe my roommate said something. He's the one who set me up with Beth in the first place. Or maybe she drove by my apartment that night and saw you through the window. *How* she found out doesn't really matter, does it?"

"Maybe not. But Colin, I can't believe she never told me any of this. Especially her suspicions about Lara."

That had surprised him, too. "I wonder how she figured it out."

"Looking back, I can't believe I *didn't*. Since we received the DNA results, I've been going through our photo albums and the resemblance is obvious. She's so much like you, Colin, it's almost spooky."

"I wonder if Lara will ever be okay with that?"

"It's still early days for her. Especially now that she has Neil's conviction to deal with. Attempted murder is not a minor charge. It'll be a long time before Lara's life feels normal again."

He remembered the way she had cried and cried in his arms the day it happened. He'd felt so protective of her then. And still did. "It's our job to help speed the process."

"Yes." Sally sighed. "I still find it hard to believe Beth kept such a big secret to herself."

"It must have been a burden," Colin agreed. Unlike Sally, he'd had some time to mull this over. At first he'd wondered what his life would have been like if Beth had handled the situation differently. But eventually he'd realized nothing could be gained by that sort of conjecture. He and Beth had been happy, but now she was gone and it was time to move on.

In her letter she effectively gave him and Sally her blessing.

Sally turned her head to the window and, seeing her in profile, Colin was reminded of the first time he'd laid eyes on her, sitting at the front of the class in Foundations to Law.

There's something about that girl, he'd thought then. And he thought the same thing now.

"Sally, will you marry me?"

"What?"

Her startled blue eyes had never looked larger.

"I love you. I'm crazy about you. Let's not lose another year, another week, another minute. Marry me, Sally, and let's spend the rest of our lives together."

"Oh, Colin." She covered her face with her hands, then placed them in his. "I don't see that there's anything to say but *yes.*"

THE WEDDING WAS SMALL, with just Lara, and a handful of friends in attendance. They said their vows at Elbow Falls, then drove to Bragg Creek for dinner. After, Sally and Lara helped Colin move a few carloads of his possessions to their house. Sally had promised Colin half of her home office and a moving truck was coming the next Monday to haul his desk, favorite chair and filing cabinets.

The rest of his furniture and belongings he was putting up for sale, along with the house.

Sally appreciated his generosity in moving to her house for Lara's sake. She also appreciated her daughter's reciprocal sweetness. Right after the service, she'd given Colin a hug and said, "I guess a girl can never have too many dads, huh?"

That had brought tears to Colin's eyes. And hers, too.

Sally had extended her leave from work by a week to take care of the wedding and its aftermath. Now, she was preparing the first dinner that she, Colin and Lara would share as a family. She was making a pork tenderloin stir-fry and had all the ingredients ready on the cutting board by the stove. She turned on the gas to heat the wok, then heard something from the back door.

A moment later, Colin burst in with a boxful of his old skiing trophies. "Lara said she wanted to see these. Where should I put them?"

Sally rolled her eyes to the ceiling. "Anywhere but the mantel."

"Very funny." The phone rang and he shifted the box a few inches higher. "I'm expecting a call from a client. Can you answer that, please? I'll put this in the office and be right back."

Sally lowered the heat on the stove, then reached for the portable phone on the counter. At just that moment, Lara barreled in with Armani, and Colin reemerged from the study. On the second ring, she pressed the talk button.

"Hello?"

"May I speak to Sally Stowe, please?"

"Speaking."

"Please hold for the federal minister of justice."
Sally put a hand to her throat, as her gaze flew first
to Colin, then her daughter.

"What is it?" Colin asked, his expression suddenly solemn. Lara, too, appeared worried as she
moved in closer to her stepfather.

Sally shook her head, unable to believe this was
really happening to her. Wasn't there a limit to how
much good fortune one person should be entitled to?
Days ago she'd married the man she knew she'd
been meant to share her life with. Her daughter, her
beautiful daughter, was healthy and happy and
stronger than Sally had ever given her credit for.

That was enough. Really, it was more than
enough.

"What is it, Sally?" Colin asked again.

This time she told him. "I'm on hold for the minister of justice."

"Holy cow." He turned to Lara. "Did you hear
that? Your mother's going to be a judge."

It was true, Sally thought, still holding, knowing
she would hold for an hour if it took that long. She
was going to be a judge. And she'd been so sure the
appointment was beyond her grasp…

She glanced again at Colin. Just as she'd been so

sure, not that long ago, that the man she loved would be forever unattainable, as well.

"Thank you," she whispered, not sure who she was speaking to, just knowing she had to say the words out loud. But then she fell silent as a man started to speak on the other end of the line. After he finished, Sally replied in a strong, firm voice. "Yes, Minister. I will be honored to accept the appointment."

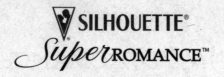

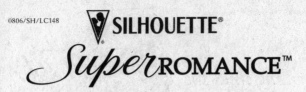

SILHOUETTE®
*Super*ROMANCE™

*A brand new series in which life will
never be the same again!*

HOMETOWN GIRL *by Margaret Watson*
August 2006

AN ACCIDENTAL FAMILY
by Darlene Graham
September 2006

FAMILY AT LAST *by KN Casper*
October 2006

HOME FOR CHRISTMAS *by Carrie Weaver*
November 2006

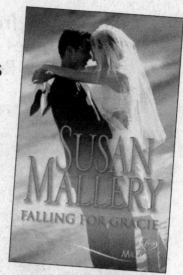

FREE

2 BOOKS AND A SURPRISE GIFT!

We would like to take this opportunity to thank you for reading this Silhouette® book by offering you the chance to take TWO more specially selected titles from the Superromance™ series absolutely FREE! We're also making this offer to introduce you to the benefits of the Mills & Boon® Reader Service™—

- ★ **FREE home delivery**
- ★ **FREE gifts and competitions**
- ★ **FREE monthly Newsletter**
- ★ **Books available before they're in the shops**
- ★ **Exclusive Reader Service offers**

Accepting these FREE books and gift places you under no obligation to buy; you may cancel at any time, even after receiving your free shipment. Simply complete your details below and return the entire page to the address below. You don't even need a stamp!

YES! Please send me 2 free Superromance books and a surprise gift. I understand that unless you hear from me, I will receive 4 superb new titles every month for just £3.69 each, postage and packing free. I am under no obligation to purchase any books and may cancel my subscription at any time. The free books and gift will be mine to keep in any case.

U6ZEE

Ms/Mrs/Miss/Mr..Initials ....
BLOCK CAPITALS PLEASE

Surname ....

Address ....

....

....Postcode ....

Send this whole page to:
The Reader Service, FREEPOST CN81, Croydon, CR9 3WZ